The Après-Ski Proposal

by

Cassandra Joelle

For my dad.

I hope you are skiing again in heaven.

Table of Contents

Chapter 1

December 10th

That night was the night; that I was *sure* of. My boyfriend of fourteen months, Theo McCain, was going to propose. My big 30th was the next day, but that night, he told me he was coming by for something very important, and there was only one thing that could mean.

I'd been praying for that day since we had met: the day my charming prince would ask me to be his wife. Knowing Theo, a world-class ski jumper, we'd have a mountain top elopement. He'd be wearing a black tuxedo and I, a long, dramatic billowing white gown. We'd trek up there in a bright, red gondola, sipping fizzy drinks and talking excitedly about our future together. The only thing that remained to fulfill my fantasy was the ring and with the Lord's blessing, I would soon get it.

After scouring my closet for just the right look, I settled on a raspberry silk blouse tucked into black jeans. Theo was a formal dresser, being out in the public eye and had been heavily influencing my closet over the past year. Before him, you could have caught me strictly in baggy clothes on weekends— no zippers or tight waistlines. In contrast, I felt like I'd just stepped off a private plane.

While I'd been hinting at it for months, Theo hadn't taken the bait but would just smile when I spoke of it. He wasn't the type of guy who gushed at his dreams or plans to take over the world, but I had been fine with that and adapted to his personality. There was nothing I wanted more in life than a family of my own— a happy home full of love with beautiful children, darling pets, and a handsome husband. And I wanted that husband to be Theo.

Theo was a gem, and I couldn't wait to see him step into the role of husband and father. Since losing his own parents at a young age and being raised by his grandparents, family was even higher on his list of priorities. I didn't know how I'd gotten so lucky with that man who was not just charming, talented and drop-dead-gorgeous, but also a man who wanted a family as much as I did.

I styled my strawberry blonde hair perfectly with a gentle curl, half up. Theo had always been complimentary of that style, often gushing over how nice it looked, so I knew to do it for such a special occasion like that day. My makeup was dramatic, though it was only four in the afternoon. I opted for a dark, sparkly eyeshadow and coordinating raspberry lipstick. But nothing was as perfect as my nails were; thank goodness, I got in for a last-minute manicure that morning. I swooned at the thought of Theo taking my hand in his at any moment.

For the ring itself, I didn't care one bit what it looked like. Even if it was made of tinfoil, I would have still said "yes" and worn it for the rest of my life. Theo was a little more fashion forward than I was, often sporting the best brands that I'd never heard of through his sponsorships or influencer deals, but I didn't know what that meant for a ring. During our shopping trips or strolls throughout town, we often walked past the jewelry stores, and he entertained my looking in the windows. While diamonds were undeniably beautiful, I saw the ring as a symbol of love and commitment; I told him repeatedly I needed nothing flashy. A simple band was all that I needed.

The truth was, we'd talked about our future so frequently, or at least I had brought it up, that it felt surreal since things were finally happening. I felt ecstatic as I considered the ways he might propose. Would he take me somewhere? Would he do it right there in my condo with the view of the mountains behind us? Would we snuggle on the couch in excitement as he recounted what my father had said when he asked him for my hand?

I thought of my parents whom I hadn't heard from in a few days. Theo had asked their permission, right? My mother's inability to keep a secret if her life depended on it made it surprising that she could keep that from me. As someone who didn't like surprises, I would have preferred to know if it wasn't so obvious, that was.

When the knock came, I barely contained my excitement. I put on my best smile and opened the door. His face made my heart drop. He didn't greet me with joy, happiness, or even kindness; in fact, he looked downright *miserable*.

If I was honest with myself, he had been miserable often lately, but his moods were quick to pass, and I never let them affect me. I was just happy to be with him even if he *was* constantly away, off competing in championships or training. I never asked for much, and I had learned expectations were better left behind. Early on, I decided I would always let Theo come to me, never being needy or demanding anything from him, because his schedule was already so strained with obligations. I didn't want our relationship to feel like another task for him. And it worked swimmingly that far, so why did he look like that at that time?

"H-hey, Theo." His body language was stiff, standoffish. When I stepped out of the doorway, signaling for him to enter, he lingered in the hallway for a moment too long, like whatever he wanted to do, he thought he may stay out there. I took a deep breath and held it in. *Nerves are to be expected when making a life altering decision,* I told myself. But my excitement at the events I thought would happen that evening quickly began dwindling, and a pit in my stomach took its place.

When he finally entered my condo, he didn't remove his shiny blue designer coat. The paranoia he had about getting a tear or stain on that thing was laughable but made sense considering he wore it as part of a sponsorship deal that he had with the company. Even if Theo got into a vehicle, he removed it first, holding it in his lap to protect it. That told me one thing: *He wasn't planning on staying very long.*

After standing for at least several minutes, Theo paced. While I was never usually the first to speak, having adapted to his very calculated and aloof personality, I couldn't take it anymore. "What's up? What's *wrong?*"

"SkySki in Canada has given me the opportunity to be represented by their company for the entire season. It's my dream come true."

My jaw dropped. "Oh, okay." I digested his announcement while still searching for the downside. "That's great news, Theo! Congratulations." I tried to picture how that would work, being away from him for… weeks? Months? The ski season lasted until *April* in some regions. With no vacation time left, it appeared I would have to choose to follow him or keep my job. "So, work is a little rocky right now, but I'll try to work out a way to come see you."

"No, Claire. I'm leaving, and I…" He trailed off, appearing to have some stitch of emotion wash over him, if only for a moment. He pointed to me and back to himself with his finger as he spit out the words, "I want to end things with us."

"What?" I released a laugh because it seemed so absurd. We had been perfectly in love for fourteen months and yet… Hadn't we? And yet he was… breaking up with me? I swallowed the lump in my throat.

"Look, I'm sorry, but it's not just this tour in Canada that changes things for me. I've thought about this for a long time. We want different things, Claire. I'm the adventurous type. You're more of a homebody. I want to be up at dawn summiting a mountain and… Well, you don't even like to ski."

It was true. I wasn't a skier. Though I grew up in the shadow of my father, Mac Riley, arguably the most famous downhill skier of all time, I never formally gave skiing a chance, and then I felt like I'd missed my window of opportunity– like I was too old to start. So, when I met Theo and he knew who my dad was, he just assumed not only was I also a talented skier, but that I craved time on the slopes as much as he and my dad did. Theo idolized my father in a way that, at first, I found flattering. But as time went on, the comparison between my father and me only added strain on our relationship. Still, things had been progressing wonderfully with Theo, and I never in a million years saw that coming.

"But we can like different things, Theo. I support you on your adventures, don't I? Who's in the front row cheering you on whenever I can? I'm at every one of your jumps that I can get to. I've never complained when you've gone out for extended periods of time. I have always patiently waited for you to return. It's been fine. I can put up with it, Theo. We are independent people. I can love you from a distance. I want you to follow your dreams in Canada with SkySki. It's my dream come true, if your dreams come true. We can lead different lives."

He looked away, his eyes focused on the view of the mountains from my condo's living room window. It had a fantastic shot of Superstition Peak, the most beautiful slope on Sage Mountain Resort because of its double tipped mountain, shaped like a small "V" at the top. Skiers from all over the world had traveled there over the years to get a picture at its summit. Before Sage Mountain Resort became a world-class ski destination, there used to be a small wooden shack at the bottom of the lift that sold t-shirts that said, "I Skied the V."

Still with his back to me, Theo shook his head as if he knew I was watching him, but then again, everyone always did. Even without his superstar status, he was a sight for sore eyes. Everyone looked his way, even platonically. Some people are so good looking that the rest of us feel we are merely in their orbit. It was true with Theo. Being with him made me feel like I was the lucky one, the reminder of which made me panic.

"Can't we be different? We could have our own lives and separate interests and meet in the middle." I felt myself pleading with him then, and desperation wasn't a good look on anyone.

"I want a partner who will do the things that I love… with me." His words were sad. Dried up. Tired. I felt myself breaking down, not just at the realization that this was over, but at how it was happening. He had reached the end in his mind, and his heart; that, I could feel.

"I don't want to be a ski-jumper. I'm afraid of heights and skiing…" I took a breath, examining hopes and dreams for my life, and now watching as they were slipping through my hands like water. "It just isn't my forte. I don't feel comfortable with it. I've been around it my whole life and I still can't pick it up. And honestly, I'm feeling a little sick and tired of snow and cold weather." I let out a laugh as a desperate plea to lighten the mood, but I was raising my voice and moving my arms wildly, which helped nothing.

We went skiing together… less than a handful of times, that was. I never left the bunny hill, and he expected me to be on the Double Black Diamonds by the time of the Last Chair, so it never ended well to say the least. There was too much pressure to ski with Theo; with anyone, really, because of who my dad was. Any slip-up or public knowledge that I was incapable of staying upright on skis was a slap in the face to anyone watching, because I had to face it— my father was an Olympian skier. My boyfriend, now ex-, was a champion ski-jumper and moving on epically with one of the top skiing brands in the world. I was the farthest thing from it.

"I just can't do this, Claire. It's over for me."

He pulled his eyes away from the window and looked back at me. Shrugging his shoulders, he immediately went to the hallway closet and pulled out a small moving box that I didn't recall being there before. We didn't live together, but since he was gone so much on his mountain adventures, it had been my idea to bring a few of his things over so that I could keep him at the top of my mind. And at first, when everything was new and exciting, it was just what he wanted to hear. He must have brought the box with him last week when he came over with takeout; I recalled all the Chinese food being in a large box, just like that. It pained me to think he'd been planning that at all.

"Did you plan this?" I was so blindsided, my words changed to accusatory.

"Look, I feel sad too. But I have made up my mind. We just aren't clicking, Claire. I wanted this to work with every fiber of my being. To be a part of your family for the last year was a dream come true. Your father is my hero, after all. Believe me, I loved you, but— ."

A phrase followed by "but" is void in my book. I also felt the past tense of *love* break my chest in two. He stopped arguing and mechanically removed the few items from the shelf and placed them in the box: pictures of his childhood pets, trinkets from his travels, and his childhood skiing trophies.

"Is there someone else?" My mind couldn't fathom that someone I loved would leave me.

He sighed, not answering immediately, which furthered the stress of that scenario. "Yes."

My heart sank. Suddenly, his face twisted in anguish, like he, too, was on the verge of tears.

"By that I mean my love for my sport."

His words came out softer, kinder than I'd ever heard from him, but I didn't know if I believed him. That whole thing felt like a setup, as if one of those hidden camera television shows could burst in from the hallway any minute and inform me that I'd just been pranked— except for one thing: the man who stood before me wouldn't do that to me. He might have wanted to end things, break my heart and leave the shattered pieces for the birds to peck at, but he wasn't a mean person.

I opened my mouth for a rebuttal but went weak. There was nowhere I could grasp from there to hold on to, and we both knew it. "I thought this was it— that we would get married and have children. I thought you were coming to propose to me."

Theo shrugged, and I knew at one time— no matter how short that time had been— he thought so, too. But after fourteen months of dating, he learned who I was and who I wasn't.

"Claire, come on." He set the box down. "Have children? And what, stay at home when I want to take them up in the mountains? To wait at the base lodge while they take their first runs? I want to instill a love for the outdoors in my children and this– you and me? Our relationship isn't one of partnership. We don't share our life's passion. We just aren't right. And we both deserve someone who's right for us, Claire." He picked the box back up and went to the door.

His words stung, and soon the waterworks flowed freely from my eyes. I felt like such a fool crying in front of that man who had chosen to leave me. I'd accepted all his faults– and there had been many– because our love was greater than that. And I thought it was mutual. Clearly, I thought wrong.

"Please, let's talk about this. I mean, really? Tomorrow is my big thirty." I couldn't believe the words out of my mouth. Was I… begging him? Guilting him for dumping me the night before my thirtieth birthday, arguably the most important birthday I've had to date? One of the most important birthdays in a woman's life? I put my head in my hands as he left without another word, shutting the door softly behind him as if closing the door normally might have awoken the fiery beast inside of me that just wanted to scream.

Chapter 2

December 11th

I woke up with a pounding headache. My body felt drained of
its tears and desperate for a tall glass of water. Grasping for
my surroundings, I stood up from the couch that I had fallen
asleep on, still fully dressed from the night before. My face
felt disgusting from the makeup that I didn't bother to wash
off. What I needed was a long, hot bath, but first, I went to the
fridge and poured some water out of my filtered pitcher.

Pushing all the thoughts from my mind of Theo and
his greater love for the mountains than for me, I listened to
the world around me. My microwave clock read 5:59 a.m.; the
silence was deafening at that hour. My condo, one of only four
in the entire building, felt empty and lifeless. Void of joy. After

I drank the water, I went and poured myself a hot bath and rummaged through my drawers for the fancy bath salts that someone gave me for Christmas last year, the kind that would take the stress right out of my body. In doing so, I unintentionally caught my reflection. I reached for a makeup wipe and started scrubbing while I looked at the label for the "Relaxation Remedy" bath salts. It advised to use two scoops with the metal scoop provided.

As I dumped the entire contents of the container in the tub, I flipped off the bathroom light and opened the blind to my bathroom window. No one could see me in there since the bathroom window faced an open field that would one day be another luxury hotel. But at that time, it was still a slice of what the Sage Mountain of my childhood used to be: vast and wild.

Watching the sunrise come up over the hill was therapeutic. I thought about God and His promises to me, to everyone. *He only gives a person what they can handle, and I know I can move on from this…* Eventually, I closed my eyes as a few more tears escaped, saying a prayer for healing, happiness, and His supernatural peace to wash over me.

Lord, I only want what is in your divine plan for my life. While I would love for that to include Theo, You know all the days of my life, and Your plan is far greater than anything I could ever imagine. Lord, please comfort me during this horrendous time. Thank You for the many blessings in my life. And I know You are here with me in my heartache. Lord, please help me. Give me Your hand and guide me. I feel hopeless and lost.

I awoke to the sound of my phone ringing. Sitting up, I concluded the bath salts worked, as I'd fallen back asleep in the tub during my prayer. Because of that, hypothermia was about to set in. Oh, dear. What time was it? The sun was up, as a shimmering light came washing in through the window, touching everything inside of my bathroom. Stepping out of the tub, I went for my towel and plush robe while heading to see who was trying to call me.

Crushingly, it wasn't Theo calling to tell me he'd made a terrible mistake. I knew it had only been hours since he ended it, but I yearned for a time when it wouldn't hurt like that anymore. The caller was my mother.

"Hey, mom." My voice was raspy and weak. She hesitated, knowing something was off, but asked if she could swing by to drop off a little something special from her and Dad. "Sure, I'm home. I'd love to see you guys." They would be there in twenty minutes, and I had a miracle to perform on my eyes and desperately needed to tidy up before then.

I went into my room and threw on a pair of warm socks, stretch jeans, and a baggy t-shirt, something I wore pre-Theo all the time. I also dabbed on a quick swipe of concealer under my eyes and a brushing of waterproof mascara on my eyelashes. That enhanced my face quickly, and I looked almost normal. Thankfully, my hair was still neat from the day before, just a little flat from sleeping on it.

Taking stock of the living area, it felt like sadness and smelled like stale air. I picked up the wad of tissues from the coffee table and wiped down all the flat surfaces with a gently fragranced multi-purpose cleaner. Last, I cracked open the kitchen window ever so slightly for some fresh air. It felt much better, then.

Still having a handful of minutes, I put on an old record that I used to play on repeat until I met Theo and found out it was his least favorite type of music. I was thinking that

I had made a lot of sacrifices which he didn't ask me to make. He never told me once that I couldn't dress like this or couldn't listen to that. But I did them– cut things I loved out of my life because I wanted Theo to fit so perfectly into the void, to slide into the role of my future husband. My thoughts consumed me when another knock came at the door, causing shivers to run down my spine.

"Happy birthday, dear!" Both of my parents stood at the entryway to my condo holding balloons, a card, and a cake with the candles already in it. "We hope this is a good time. You haven't been answering your phone all morning, so we didn't get to give you much notice…"

My mother looked me up and down. "Of course, come in! It's kind of a funny story… I wasn't feeling that great, so… I took a bath, and I guess I fell asleep in it. I didn't realize how tired I was."

Playfully smacking my forehead with the palm of my hand, I chose to purposely omit the part where Theo, the guy they loved to the moon and back, had just hours before dumped me. My parents looked at me and at each other, while I eagerly motioned them inside.

"Welcome to thirty! You'll only get more exhausted from here," my mother exclaimed, laughing. "We won't keep you, dear. We know you are working today, and I'm sure you have plans at some fancy restaurant with Theo later. But we couldn't let today go by without letting you know we love you and wish you all the best for this new decade in your life."

I quickly played off my tears as being sentimental, caused by a multitude of reasons. As my father set the cake on the table, he galloped to the window to check out the mountain view.

"Thank you! I love you both so much. You're so good to me." I picked up my feet to retrieve the serving ware from my kitchen, grabbing a set of matching plates.

In the open concept condo that had little a footprint, I could see my parents shuffling around. My mother went to the record player. "I just love this record. I'm so glad you inherited my taste in music."

"Patsy, you know you love my music, especially The Beach Boys. I remember you being the one to put on their Christmas album on the way over here."

"Okay, fine. After thirty-one years of marriage, meaning I've had the chance to listen to them day in and day out, I'll admit it: They are my favorite band. Happy now?"

As I smiled at their bantering, my heart stopped noticing the time was a quarter to noon. On a Monday. Another panic set in as I had yet to contact work that I was unable to do anything that day but be a sad lump on the couch. Knowing how strict they were about professionalism, I asked my parents if they would like a cup of coffee with cake. I turned the faucet on to fill my pot, swiftly texting my boss Patricia that I'd had a major personal emergency, and I couldn't work that day. I apologized profusely, ensuring it was short, distinct, and clear, but not overly emotional to discourage any inclination on her part to pry or refuse. It was a fine line to tow, asking for a personal day when that day was already half over.

My mother was standing behind me in the kitchen when I turned around to the small island. "I brought the cake in here to cut. Don't feel you need to entertain us, dear, if you've got something else going on…? It sure is good to see you, Claire. And if there *is* something going on, I want you to feel you can tell me."

She must have been implying my appearance looked ragged and puffy. I'd never felt so awful in my life, so I was certain my looks matched that tenfold. "No, no. This is amazing. Do you want me to cut and serve the cake?"

She happily obliged and served it on three little blue plates with a white scalloped edge.

Pouring the coffee into matching cups with saucers made me feel better about my life. At least my house was in order. I took a sip of the hot coffee as I felt groggy and out of it; *I need this to kick in fast.* We all grabbed our coffee and cake and went to my dining room table directly on the other side of my kitchen wall.

"Oh, there's one thing I forgot. Mac? The gift." My mother reached for the gift bag that I hadn't noticed before now, handing it to me. "Open it." She was beaming her beautiful smile.

"You guys didn't have to get me anything. That's so sweet." I reached in, finding a beautiful black cashmere sweater. It was classy and timeless, feeling stunning in my hands, and I couldn't wait to put it on. "I absolutely love it! I'm eager to wear it right now!"

As I entered my bedroom, I fought against more tears. "Lord, please grant me the strength to get through this. I want to hold my composure... They don't need to see my pain." I took a set of deep breaths and put on the sweater in place of my baggy, formless t-shirt. Maybe it was the return to normalcy, and I wasn't sure I was ready to admit it, but that form-fitting, dressy sweater made me feel better instantly and lifted my spirits in ways I couldn't have imagined.

"There she is!" my father hollered as I stepped out of my room. I put my hands up and did a twirl for him as I had always done when I was a little girl, putting on my frilliest princess dress and modeling it for my parents. It was especially something that my father always got a kick out of.

"That looks like someone made it specifically for you, Claire."

I gave my mother a hug, thanking her for such a lovely gift and saw that in my absence, she had lit the cake up with birthday candles.

"Now, for the cake."

We all sat down for the fresh coffee and the beautiful raspberry and white chocolate cake, my favorite flavor. I blew out the darling little pink candles, robotically licking the frosting off the bottoms, and dove in. "This cake is everything." After taking that first bite, I couldn't stop. "I think I'll have another piece." My mother looked at me with a wide smile when I said that. I had been on a pretty strict diet the last year, mimicking what Theo ate, which comprised little to no carbs, fats or anything mildly enjoyable. "This might be the best cake I've ever had."

My father laughed in agreement. "It is quite delicious." He winked at my mother. "You did good, Patsy."

"What can I say? I know where to shop, Mac." She got up and refilled her coffee, offering the same to us.

"I'll take another cup, though there's enough sugar in this cake to keep me going for a few hours, before I crash, anyway."

She chuckled and returned to the table with the coffeepot, setting it on a placemat after refilling it. "So, tell us dear, where is Theo taking you tonight? I hope he is keeping up the tradition of ice skating, since you've gone for every birthday your entire life." She put her hands under her chin, reminiscent of wanting to hear the popular gossip from a gal pal.

My mother was so cute with her flaming red hair and rosy cheeks. I could not upset her yet. I needed to put that conversation off for now until I could properly handle it without crying. While I hadn't forgotten about my tradition of ice skating, I hadn't yet considered doing it solo. "Oh, I don't know. But I would *love* to check out that new Italian restaurant in Corks Canyon sometime. Maybe all three of us could do that one weekend?" It wasn't a lie, but it wasn't entirely transparent, either. I just wasn't ready to relive what had happened. To my relief, they loved that idea.

"How about when we get back from Alaska? We are heading up there soon for the new 'Badger Basin' ski lift dedication at Mystic Mountain Resort, and your father is going to be testing it out repeatedly."

She laughed, taking out her phone calendar to check the dates, and I looked at them with admiration. *This is love.* While my parents had different ideas of fun— my father's ideal time was anything on skis, and my mother's was anything with a crochet hook— they still were perfect for each other.

"We return right after New Year's. Would that work, sweetie? That gives us a couple of weeks to make the plans.

We could even get some hotel rooms and stay the weekend. I'll bet Theo would like to climb that mountain in Corks. Mac, what is it called again?" My father pondered the question, but before he could answer, I interjected.

"Let's keep it just the three of us. I never get you both to myself anymore." My father gazed at me with a quizzical look, but didn't push it. I was certain that was disappointing for him, as he loved Theo deeply, but it was what it was.

"Are you sure you'll be alright for Christmas this year? We don't want you to feel abandoned since we will spend it in Alaska." My father watched me with every word he spoke.

"Yes, I'll be fine. With all the work I'd been doing for the airport, I was actually looking forward to an extra day off that month." My parents asked a handful of questions about the progress of the airport, and we shared many polite platitudes. After we finished our coffee, they got up to leave.

"We have to take in the car for its winter tires this afternoon, so we better get going." My father stopped in front of his Olympian Wheaties Box framed poster I had of him on my wall. "You could do much better than this thing for art, dear. What about a nice, colorful landscape? An oil painting of a valley of wildflowers? I'd be happy to help you pick out something a little more hip and stylish," he teased me, and I leaned in for a hug.

The second they left, I let out a silent cry. My chest hurt from the carbs, sugar, and pain causing my anxiety levels to peak even higher. I picked up the picture of Theo on my shelf, surprised he didn't take it with his belongings, as he gave it to me when we started dating. It was almost funny to think about then, but I loved it, and it had been there on my shelf ever since. In the photo, he was donning a vintage one-piece ski suit from the 1980s. It was quite colorful and had neon pieces sewn in random patterns. He wasn't smiling but had more of a smirk as he stared into the camera. I pondered at the question: Was he ever genuinely happy with me, and if so, what changed?

Holding the photo, I felt as if he'd left it behind on purpose so I could mourn him. Suddenly, I wanted to throw the frame, break a window, and have it land on another continent. But I refrained; instead, I pulled open the door to the hallway closet that Theo had become so comfortable using and set it inside, face down on an emptied shelf.

A feeling of resentment pulsed through my veins. *Lord, please don't let me go down this path. No matter what, I do not want to feel hatred towards others*, I prayed silently. No matter what, the feelings I had for Theo were real and very raw. It was going to be an emotional rollercoaster… But I hated to feel like I was constantly on the brink of a nervous breakdown.

The sugar from the cake hit me all at once, so I found the strength to clean up the kitchen, coffee area, and dining table. Then, returning to the couch, I fluffed up the pillows and shook out the throw blanket. Absentmindedly retrieving my phone, I saw a reply from Patricia acknowledging my personal day as well as the two missed calls from my parents, but nothing else.

I lay on the couch until darkness came again, replaying the scene from the day before over and over in my mind. Despite all of it, I still expected Theo to contact me in some form that day. I checked my social media apps, but there was just well wishes from friends. No texts had come through. I even checked my seldom-used personal email… Nothing. Did Theo even care that it was my birthday?

Pain came again later when I saw Theo had updated his profile picture on social media from one of us to a photo of just him. With Theo's notoriety, he had thousands of followers on all of his accounts, but only this one he kept for family and friends, so I felt the jab from it. Though we had never publicly declared online to be in a relationship as he always preferred to keep his private life private, it was clear. He was back on the prowl.

I couldn't fathom returning to work the next day. I didn't care what it meant for my job. My only care at the time was getting over the hurt and heartbreak. Closing my social media apps, I sent Patricia an email saying that I would be out the rest of the week.

*****

As the sun slowly slid behind the peaks of Sage Mountain, I was growing tired of wallowing in my pity party. I had the rest of the week to do so, since I'd already called out of work… And it was my birthday. Ever since I could remember, that day of the year ended on ice skates, so that's what I grudgingly set out to do.

The rink was a quarter mile from home. Though it was bitter cold, I layered up as best I could, while still retaining movement, gearing up in red snow overalls and a white thermal with a heavy black sweater over it. I topped it with a down parka. Slipping into my snow boots, I walked the distance, hoping the exercise would warm me up along the way.

When I arrived, the same family who ran the rink since I was a child was there to greet me, but instead of having their children there, they pointed out to me a new grandchild. "That's little Flora. Isn't she adorable? Already on skates– my heart." Paul clutched his chest and smiled, while his wife, Philippa, handed me a pair of skates.

"Happy birthday, Claire."

"How did you remember? Gosh, I just love you two. Thank you."

"You have the same birthday as our oldest, Sheree. I remember when you were both little girls out here skating together. Now, you're all grown up."

I reminisced while she spoke. "I remember that. How is Sheree? Is this her daughter, Flora?"

Philippa shook her head. "No. Sheree has two beautiful children, Samuel and Ashley, but they live in Colorado. They will be here for Christmas."

My heart warmed knowing that Sheree had a family of her own, but it also served as yet another reminder that I was still waiting for my turn. I thanked them for the skates and turned to the rink.

Lacing up my skates and putting my snow boots out of the way under the bench, I did a familiar hobble onto the platform to get to the ice. The rink was gorgeous under the starry night sky; trees covered in twinkling lights surrounded it. Paul and Philippa served hot chocolate and apple cider while kids roasted marshmallows at the adjacent fire pits. I could hear a piano playing nearby, but I couldn't figure out where it was coming from.

I did a few trips around the rink and thought about my life; wondering if I had done anything differently, would it have created another outcome? I supposed in a sense, yes, it would have if I had left the state for college and never returned. Had I majored in art history, I could have become a professor. If I had taken up skiing when I was young, maybe I would have been following Theo to Canada. If I had chosen any of those options, it was possible that I would have been scaling mountains on that very day in the Swiss Alps with my husband, whom I met in college, and the children we had right after getting married. I wouldn't have been at the ribbon cutting with my father and never would have met Theo. Or would I had? Would I have flown in, no matter what, to be there when my father got the honors of cutting the ribbon by my hometown community? Could I really have chosen a different path and pursued things that I wasn't passionate about? I didn't think so.

I realized I had zero regrets about Theo. He was a part of my life, and I wouldn't change a thing about it except for the heartbreak I was feeling then. Oh, how I longed for it to pass. If only things could have been different for us.

Remembering God and His promises for my life, these were things I didn't need to be worrying about. I couldn't change the outcome of what had already happened. I could only continue to pray for what could be.

A few couples skated past me, holding hands. It made me think of Theo, of course, but since he had been out of town last year on my birthday, I had no memories of him there with me, to which I felt relieved. That was my tradition, after all— something I'd done countless years alone. And I was doing it again.

A gentle snow fell around me, the snowflakes kissing my face. The world was quiet as I took smooth strides around the rink, enjoying the peace of the snow and the magical element that it brought as it fell all around me. A feeling of gratefulness burst through my heart. "Thank you, God, for the beauty of your creation."

After twenty minutes, my core and legs felt warmed up, but my ears and nose felt like they might be on the verge of breaking off if I didn't step into a warm building. I exited the rink, swapping out my skates and feeling pleased that I not only checked that box, but I fully enjoyed its festive atmosphere and community. I drank a cup of hot cider with Paul and Philippa at their stand next to the warmth of the heat lamp, but I still could not warm up. Then, the piano music got louder.

"Where is that coming from?" I asked Philippa, while Paul assisted a happy, young couple with their skates.

"That's the new piano bar, just over there. See?" She pointed to a brick building with white trim. "With the people walking in… that one."

"A piano bar? I didn't know we had such a thing. Hmm. Sounds kind of fun."

"You should go check it out. Let me live through you, as we are stuck here until ten. Have fun, Claire. It's your birthday."

At her orders, I went directly there, just one block up. I didn't let myself think about it, or I would have talked myself out of it.

When I entered the dimly lit piano bar, I was surprised to see that it was exactly what it appeared to be: a bar with a piano in the center. A woman greeted me at the door.

"Good evening. Will you be listening or playing tonight?"

My eyes got wide. "I will be, um… listening. I mean, I played piano as a kid, but… listening."

She smiled and pointed to a little table in the center of the room. "Why don't you sit right there, and Andrea will come over to check on you momentarily."

I hung my coat up on the rack and took my seat. Andrea came over immediately, to which I put in an order for any hot drink she had.

"We make our own artisan cider with organic apples from Eastern Wyoming. Would you like some?"

I agreed, and she left. The woman from the front of the bar took the mic as the piano player finished his tune.

"Let's give a round of applause to Tom for his rendition of 'Take Me Out to the Ballgame'!" The crowd wildly cheered him on. "Next up, we have Jason and the player of his choice."

The man whom I presumed was Jason stood up and dramatically scanned the crowd, picking out a woman who was sitting in a booth with several others.

"Okay, Jason. You two will need to play a duet of 'Auld Lang Syne.'" The pair looked at each other in panic as they exchanged words in rapid fire. Once they started playing, it was clear that one person really had the ability, and the other one had never seen a piano before. It was quite fun, and despite some off notes, the song was recognizable.

Once that song was over, and I was on my second mug of cider served in a giant pottery mug that fit the vibe, the announcer was busy with seating a large group, and another man took his turn. I could only see the back of him as he played a solo song, a wildly inaccurate rendition of 'Fur

Elise,' but it was charming, nonetheless. Despite my five years of piano lessons, the only keys I'd touched in the last fifteen years were on my computer's keyboard, so I cringed when I thought of my ability.

The announcer returned with her soft microphone. "Thank you, sir. Please choose from the crowd, as you'll be doing a duet."

When he turned, I saw his face for the first time. We made eye contact the instant he turned around, and it didn't dawn on me that I should look away or get up and leave. But when he pointed right at me, my mind went blank.

"Wait, what? Me?" I shook my head. "I told the woman I wasn't playing tonight."

When the man got closer, his beautiful face came into focus as he offered to change his choice. "If you'd rather not, I can choose someone else."

He had a handsomely, unusual appearance with auburn hair and olive skin. His freckles looked like a map to the hidden universe of my soul. He had striking, green eyes. Did I really have a reason to say no? It *was* my birthday, after all, and it would be a memorable experience. If I said no to this chance experience, what were those five years of piano lessons really for?

"Okay, sure. I'll do it." A few claps escaped from the people sitting around me as I got up, walked over to the piano, and felt the cushion of the seat creak below our weight. *Lord, please keep this seat from falling.* I giggled at the thought of my plea to God, as the announcer came up with our assignment, and it was then that I saw she did so by picking out a random song from a large fishbowl filled with folded up pieces of paper.

"You two will play 'Chopsticks.'" The previous players groaned at our easier assignment, while the man beside me leaned in.

"We totally lucked out. There's only one of those in the fishbowl each night. Do you know it? If you don't, you can follow my lead."

I nodded my head. "I know it. I just have to warm up. You start, and I'll follow." And he did.

I couldn't help but notice how his agile hands moved across the keys like they were floating above them. After he started, my mind remembered the tune while my fingers started playing keys. The hair on the back of my neck stood up at the first few notes. I stayed on one side of the piano, but slowly, my hands reached further towards his side, reaching for the keys my heart remembered. He closed his eyes while he played, and I peeked at the man more than once. I missed a few keys, but he kept going, only smiling as he smoothed out the song with the right notes. Finally, by accident, our hands touched while we reached for the same key. Instead of moving, he put his hand over mine and we both hit the key, sending an electrical spark from my hand to my heart.

When the song was over, I felt emotion wash over me. It wasn't just that it was a lovely song, but it was a novel experience. Though we were in a room full of strangers, I felt like we were the only two people in the world. I didn't know that man, nor was I prepared to know him, but his presence felt empowering to me. Just being near him was healing for my broken heart.

He stood up and reached his hand out to shake mine. "Thank you for the song."

Seeing his face was the equivalent of staring into the sun, and I felt silly for being overcome with emotion then. I shook his hand quickly and smiled, feeling awkward at what to say. He shuffled his feet and motioned to his table off to the side, and I looked to see who his friends were. They looked like a fun group, all smiles as they looked over at us.

"Thanks for choosing me." I did a curtsy. "I'll let you get back to your table." Not hearing any objections to my words, I turned to leave but saw his *lingering* out of the corner of my eye as I paid my tab at the bar. I stole one more glance over my shoulder and caught him back at his table. He was sitting at the edge, looking in another direction. Despite his attractiveness and the fun experience, I wasn't ready to jump into his friend group and chat. My social battery had drained and left me feeling exhausted. My eyes were puffy and my sinuses were blocked from crying.

As I walked home, I said a prayer about that man, whoever he was, that maybe we would cross paths again.

Chapter 3

December 22nd

"I'm sorry I'm late! I hope I haven't kept you waiting long."

"No problem, Claire. It's only been three minutes." Anna gave off a cool smirk as she stirred some cream into her coffee. "Have a seat. I can't wait to hear how your week is going."

"Well, I'm afraid I have even less to report this time around. I probably shouldn't have even come in unless I had something worthy of therapy." *Not to mention the $120 an hour rate,* I thought to myself.

"Everything we've been working on is worthy."

I nodded in reply. Anna was right; I had come a long way in my emotional processing and walk with Christ since I started counseling. While I had been attending counseling less frequently over the last year since being so happy and distracted with Theo, Anna received my SOS call and immediately scheduled me for three sessions following the breakup. But every time I entered there, I was at a loss for words, and she had to manually get me talking.

"Now," Anna sat on the couch across from me, pulling out her notes and the Bible. "What's happened so far today?" She smiled at me coyly, ready for the waterfall of words to pour from my mouth.

It worked like a charm, and within seconds, I was replaying the mundane details of my morning routine to her, that if I hadn't shared them, they would go undetected and forgotten from history. And every time I went through the recounting of the moments, I'd recall why I was there in the first place.

"Theo just brutally blindsided me by dumping me. I feel like a failure and like I'm starting over in life. It doesn't help that by the time my dad was thirty, he was an Olympian. I don't know what to do, where to start, or how to take control of my life anymore. But I know I need to do something soon. I am desperate to do something… anything… significant." Saying it aloud to someone I was paying handsomely was simple, but these were things that I could never share with a friend. Not that I had very many of them around those days. Since my town was being bought up piece by piece by a ski conglomerate, almost everyone had moved away to cheaper, greener pastures.

"What exactly do you feel you need to *do*?"

"Either tackle something at a big level, or maybe marry someone who has? I don't know. It's pathetic to hear the words come out, especially since I very well know neither of those things is going to happen." I slumped my chin into my fist and sighed.

"And why is that? You're still young."

"Turning thirty felt very… finite. I swear I hear a violin playing in the background music that is my life's soundtrack, as if my life is a movie. It should be a flirty romantic comedy, but it's shaping up to be a Shakespearean tragedy. I just feel like anything I start now is going to be lame."

Anna took her pen to paper, rapidly scribbling down notes. "You are the only one setting that standard for yourself, Claire. It seems to me that you're putting your father on a pedestal where no one should be except God. The idolization of man is sinful. Don't get me wrong; we are to love one another, but not worship. I want you to pray about this immediately."

Was I… idolizing? I reflected on her words for a moment. "I don't know if I would call it that… I just want to be like him, date someone he likes, make life choices he will approve of…" I trailed off, then seeing that it was *exactly* what I'd been doing. *Lord, you are so patient with me.* "Yikes, you're totally right, Anna. I've put my father at a god-like level. I never would've considered that unless you said something, so thank you."

"Hmm. You told me once that your dad never pushed you to ski because he wanted you to find your own thing… And you didn't exactly beg him to. What happened to that? What is *your* thing?"

I put my head in my hands. "That's the problem. I don't have my own hobbies. I just think that had I started when I was a kid, it *could have been* my thing."

"Could'a, would'a, should'a, Claire. You know what I always say… It's the devil who wants us to regret. God is in the present. What do you feel He is leading you towards? What do you think God wants for your life?"

"I know He led me to help with the youth group at church. And that has given me so much fulfillment. I just love helping the church, and the teens are a blast." There was something really special about being around teenagers. I connected with them on a different wavelength because, even though I was older, I felt like my emotional growth had been stunted due to not marrying or having kids of my own. Despite feeling like a teenager myself, the only difference was that I could eat cake without permission. I shrugged it off. I had felt lost for quite some time. "I know it sounds cliché, and not very 'progressive' of me, but I really thought I would be married by now. The fact I'm not married feels like one more disappointment."

"That's not true. You still have plenty of time for that. I didn't get married until I was thirty-seven. I know the struggles of waiting. But I promise you, it's worth the wait if it means you find the right partner— someone who adds to your life and brings you joy, not someone who takes joy away."

I took a deep breath, believing her as my eyes moved over to the wedding picture on her desk. I picked it up, analyzing it for the secrets of finding someone. "I also want a family. I thought I'd have the perfect family by now: a boy and a girl, both with flaming red hair like my mother. We'd have a golden retriever named Scout. But most of all, there would be love. And I would love them no matter what they did."

"That sounds familiar." Anna put down her pen.

"How so?" I scrunched my forehead in confusion, putting the wedding picture back on her desk with no more answers than I had to start with.

"Your father never forced you into his sport, encouraging you to find your own 'thing,' and now it's easily one of your biggest grudges in life."

I released my expression. Anna was right. I held that against him, putting the blame on everyone else but me. If I was honest with myself, I would have never committed to lessons or formal solo attempts at skiing either. I consistently directed all of my blame away from myself for as far back as I could remember. "I know he loves me, and I love him. I love both of my parents. They are the best."

Anna wrote a note to herself. I was about to ask her for a copy of her notes, when I remembered something else. "And, they loved Theo. I'm just sick about breaking the news to them that Theo dumped me… I have been avoiding having that conversation at all." I hid my face in my hands.

"So, you haven't told them yet? Okay. But what's the worst thing that could happen when you do?"

My mind raced with possibilities. I had a visual of my father adopting Theo legally as his son. "I feel like they will just think I am a loser, because that's how I feel."

"No. That's how Theo made you feel. There's a difference, Claire."

Her words hit me like a stray arrow. I played with them in my mind for a moment. "Hmm. Well, getting dumped is pretty brutal, I suppose. It makes me feel... unworthy in life."

Anna nodded. "I know, but that's the devil playing his hand once again. Let me put it this way..." Anna set her notepad and pen down, using her hands to speak. "God is love. Anything that isn't love, hurt, anger, fear— that's the devil playing into our emotions. God will never make you feel those things, so if you are, you know who is."

"That's beautiful." I gave that some retrospection. "Regardless, it still hurts a lot considering I spent fourteen months with this person and really saw myself marrying him. So, part of me doesn't know how I should feel. I just wish that

God would spell it out for me. Lord, please show me what to do, tell me how to feel, and lead me to the right path."

"Did you want to marry him for the optics, or did every fiber in your being speak the language that only you and him know? When God sends us love, we know. There's a difference. The right guy vs. the right now guy is not the same. And I'm not saying every love story is a long-winded dramatic affair that could grace the pages of a romance novel, but in your heart, it might feel that way."

"Being with Theo made me feel so special. I was over the moon for him, and it *felt* like a love story. Except because it clearly wasn't mutual, that is. Sure, he dropped a few hints that he wasn't settled in life. I think he is reaching for a level of perfection that doesn't exist, at least not in my mind. However, I hoped that would eventually change."

"So, you thought you could fix him." Anna put the end of her pen to her mouth.

"Well, no. Not that. I just thought– " She cut me off.

"That wasn't a question, Claire. You felt special because someone like this 'chose you,' but he wasn't satisfied with what you offered because he's seeking something else entirely. And I'm sorry that happened. And you may not feel this way yet, but believe me, Claire… Your future husband is out there right now, waiting to meet you.”

“No, you’re right. It *does not* feel that way right now. Despite understanding what you’re saying, I can’t control it. *I miss him.* I really think he is the one for me. That *he* is my future husband.”

“Claire, everything is out of our hands. You are not in control, but God is. And that’s why we pray.”

Anna looked at me for a long time before changing the subject. I could tell she just wanted to knock some sense into me and shake me like a rag doll, but thankfully for me, she was far too kind and patient for that.

“When was the last time you had a change of scenery? Maybe that could help you get out of this funk. Even if only for a few days. With the ski season just getting ramped up and this unusually cold winter we are having, it could really change the game for you to see what else is out there before the chaos of the busy season.”

I snorted and laughed. “Like a vacation?” I hadn’t considered one for quite some time but mostly because for the last year, my life revolved around Theo. “I don’t know if I can afford one. But it does sound intriguing. I’ve always wanted to go to an island somewhere and see what it's like to be too hot for a change."

"So, we have a goal to write in our journal. Take a vacation."

She motioned to the pretty pen and paper I brought to all of my sessions, at her request, but this was the first time I realized what they were for. I wrote the three words and waited, seeing if they would make me feel better.

"Having something to look forward to is a game changer, Claire. Vacations don't have to break the bank, either. Some of the best trips I've ever taken were on a shoestring budget."

I considered renting a place a few hours away in a bigger town that had no ties to skiing or snow, but immediately felt filled with dread. It was almost like I *wanted* to be here and *wanted* to be miserable. I was about to share my self-analysis with Anna before she interjected my thoughts.

"While we're at it, let's add 'accomplish a goal' to that list. Any goal you set, of your choosing. Like you said, you feel you need to set out and do something. Claire, I believe that is God steering you towards something, and I want you to explore it."

My hands felt shaky at the idea as I wrote it down. I think I knew what that goal was, but it was far too scary to admit it out loud…yet.

"There's also a pattern I've noticed with you. You deflect some, not all, but a substantial amount of responsibility for your life onto others. We all do it, but I want you to consider it from now on. You need to take charge of your life by giving Jesus the reins. Let Him direct your steps. Let Him guide you in your day-to-day choices, not the weight of other people's opinions. Can you do that, Claire?"

I considered the question and saw she was again correct. Despite being emotionally wounded by my breakup, I had been playing the victim in many other aspects of my life, missing out on the countless opportunities I could have taken. "Giving up control is a very scary thing, Anna. I don't know if I can do it."

"I know it seems scary. But we must submit to God's will for our lives. Think of it this way: I want less of me— my choices, my decisions, my skewed logic— because I am an imperfect sinner, living in a fallen world. And I want more of

Jesus with His perfect plan for my life. Because what could be better than that?"

I shed a tear as she spoke. "I never thought of it that way before."

She jotted some notes down before flipping over to a new page. "When was the last time you spoke to your father?"

"It's been a little over a week, when my parents stopped by on my birthday, after I fell asleep in the tub." I sheepishly smiled, still feeling awkward about that encounter. A week was a long time to go without talking to family, and I knew it. "I've spoken to my mother a handful of times since, over text message, so they know I'm okay and all."

"It sounds like you owe him a phone call." Anna crossed her legs, putting the ball back in my court. "Add that to your list, too."

After I wrote it down, I felt like the wind had been sucked out of my sails. "I just want to put it off until I have something to tell him."

"Here we go with the people pleasing again. Where does this need to please him come from? Do you feel the same way about anyone else?"

“For the people pleasing aspect, no, I really don’t feel the need for anyone else but my dad. Why do I feel like I need to? That’s why I’m here.” I flashed a smile and winked at Anna, knowing I was being very unhelpful. I certainly didn’t want to shatter what hope remained for me by confessing that Theo had dumped me.

“Do you think it’s that you admire him so much that you aim to be at his level?”

“Yes, but I’m not capable of achieving anything like that now. Even if I tried to do something like taking up skiing, for instance… I’m getting too late of a start.”

“Do you want to start?”

Do I? Is that what I want? I felt relief drain from my body; someone else spoke into existence the goal that I was too afraid to write moments ago. “Yes.” I felt the lump in my throat as I explored this desire that I’d avoided for years. It wasn’t just that I wanted to, but the feelings of others’ expectations of my implied ability mixed with my own feelings of inadequacy were a lethal combo to my mental health. With Theo, there had been so much pressure to ski that I couldn’t start. With my father, he never really offered the chance.

"Claire, I give you permission to start anything you feel you need to explore. Write that down for your accomplishment: 'learn to ski.' I will even comp today to go towards your first lift ticket."

I let out a laugh and felt choked up. My emotions were always very close together, and that day, I felt one sneeze away from a nervous breakdown. "What if I can't?" I whispered.

Anna sat in silence, letting me wallow in my pity for a few seconds, before a friendly but defiant rebuttal. "What if you can?"

*****

Out in the parking lot of Anna's riverfront office building, there was a sampling of luxury cars. This was a very wealthy community, though it didn't use to be. Because of their wealth, the residents had every choice under the sun for services, so a person had to be *pretty good* at making it there. Anna was the lone Christian counselor who practiced in the town of Sage Mountain, Wyoming, and just being a half of a mile from the ski resort, I knew she was a skier herself, though she hadn't revealed that to me… yet. *She probably didn't want to rub it in.* But the roof rack of her car was a dead giveaway.

My car might as well have been neon yellow amongst the flashy assortment for as much as it stuck out. It was from the 1900s, after all— one of the few remaining relics of what used to be the normal occurrence here, not that I cared. I sighed as I climbed into my Ford Explorer; it used to be a very different place. Growing up in Sage Mountain brought many warm memories that accompanied an idyllic small-town life: ice skating on a frozen lake; sledding down steep hills and warming huts filled to the brim with neighborly warmth; and sharing wishes for the new year over cups of hot cocoa. So much had changed in Sage Mountain.

It all happened so fast. First, it was the developers who showed up like thieves in the night. They went around town, spreading the word of their fancy Town Hall meeting, where they offered huge dollar amounts for land and homes near the ski hill that promised financial security for a lifetime. Nearly half the town disappeared after that; the ones left behind called them "sell outs" and tried to fight against what was happening to our home.

There was only one problem: money. The residents didn't have it, and the developers did, meaning they had fancy lawyers and contracts waiting just in case someone wanted to say something. "I dare you to do something about it," I overheard one developer say harshly one night to a third-generation family who had homesteaded near the mountain.

Since the mine shut down, our economy took a hit, and things had been strained there. The goal for our town had been to transition into tourism, but with such slim margins to do so, the future had seemed bleak. For some, myself included, the developers were an answer to prayer, a way to keep living in Sage Mountain since they brought hundreds of new jobs in virtually all industries.

Nothing, however, could have prepared me for the change that happened before my eyes. In a matter of weeks, numerous houses were demolished. It didn't take long before they started breaking ground on new luxury hotels. Within two years, the ski place had quadrupled in size with a promise to make Sage Mountain the top resort in North America. *A promise they followed through on.*

The shadowy figure in all of this was one man whom I'd never met, but only knew that his name was James Walker.

While I didn't vilify him, as I knew change was inevitable, many of our locals did. He was the brains behind the development. It was a single stroke of his pen that essentially bought our entire town and rolled it into his ski town monopoly. He was the CEO of the company who now owned the town of Sage Mountain, its resort, and its new state-of-the-art regional airport that was currently being built. Because of that man, many of our town's families had to move because of crippling property taxes. My friends moved away, and my hometown was unrecognizable. But also because of that man, I had new job opportunities that never would have been possible otherwise. They held opening ceremonies to honor my father, recognizing him as a Sage Mountain Olympian athlete, and I found great enjoyment in some of the new amenities in town.

The only reason I could still afford to live there was because I inherited my grandmother's condo in one of the two buildings that weren't torn down, since the property was next to an "undesirable" train station. Though it had been out of service since the coal mine fire over twenty-five years ago, it was owned by a corporation that was even bigger than the ski resort developers and wisely, they knew they couldn't win that fight.

Turning over my ignition, I thought about what Anna said about my first ski ticket. *"Everyone can ski but you."* The voice of Theo rang through my mind, inflicting doubt and shame. *"Look at those kids. They don't even need poles!"* I shut down the memories of his painful words, putting my head in my hands.

> *God, are You there? It's Claire. Anna says I'm better off without Theo. I want nothing that isn't in Your plan, Lord. I don't want a man who doesn't love me. But please take the pain away. In your name, Amen.*

After several minutes of silence in my prayer, I looked up to see that my window had been defrosted. I backed out of my spot and mentally returned to my workday.

Working from home gave me more flexibility than going into an office, such as the ability to attend therapy in the middle of the day, but it seemed to only add to my loneliness at that time. Upon arriving home, I checked my inbox and found three new messages from my boss.

"Can we have a phone meeting in an hour? I need to go over this design proof for the Sage Mountain airport faux beams you put in."

"Hello? Are you working today?"

"Where are you, Claire?"

Yikes. All of them transpired over the course of an hour, and I was only absent for ninety minutes. I swiftly replied. "Hello Patricia. Forgive me for missing your email. I had an appointment, but I'm back and ready to help you. Please let me know how, at your convenience."

In what seemed like an instant later, she replied, "Seems like you have a lot of those these days. Never mind; I got it handled."

Double yikes. After Theo dumped me, and I called out for a full week, I had realized I was on thin ice, especially because it was during our finalization of the airport plans. Suddenly, the ice seemed to be fracturing. It wasn't like I had planned for this to happen.

I hesitantly replied to her email in the most respective fashion I could. "Yes, I had a personal crisis this month, and I apologize for letting that impede my ability to work. I have reflected on the absence on my timecard, and I do not expect compensation for those days or the hours I have missed since."

A handful of minutes passed, and her reply dinged out of my computer speakers. "I've taken it out of your vacation time for the year. Once your vacation time is exhausted, any days missed without a doctor's note and hospital admission slip will result in your not being welcomed back. You have one remaining day left for the fiscal year that just started October 1st, since we go with the mountain operating timeline. That means for the next 11 months, you will not be allowed paid time off, past one day."

Triple yikes. The ice was caving in. *I was about to fall through and drown.* How was I supposed to make it through the rest of the fiscal year with no… rest? The thoughts of my therapist suggesting a vacation were laughable now. I closed my email and logged onto my bank.

Checking account: $6,279.78
Savings account: $9,246.35
Average monthly spend: $1,788.92

I was in better shape than I thought, but only because of my summer bonus for all the work I did on the new Sage Mountain airport design. The design that, when approved and put into motion, would wipe out anything that remained of my once muted town in the mountains— a town that used to be so remote, the rest of our state forgot it. Even residents who only lived an hour or two away would travel to larger ski hills in opposite directions. Everything changed when the lords of snow bought our Sage Mountain Resort.

Long gone were the days the mountain functioned only Friday-Sunday, operated by volunteers who relied on a rope tow that tore up their gloves. Taking their place and deciding for our town were conglomerates who had no prior skiing knowledge. Gondolas and bubble chairs, resort-owned shops and restaurants filled the base, and with my help, a new airport would soon expand access to the masses.

I sighed, knowing my part in wiping out the last of the locals would eventually send me packing, too. I looked around. At the time, covering the taxes on my condo required half a year's wages. In my building of four units, I was the last one who hadn't sold to the highest bidder who remodeled and made them into a nightly rental. Though I had hoped to stay in

Sage Mountain, the only home I'd ever known, that apartment was my safety net because I knew one day I could sell it and make enough to buy a house somewhere else if I lost my job. I just hoped it wouldn't be so soon. It wasn't time for me to let go of it. I pulled myself out of my work funk and walked over to the window that overlooked the newly constructed tram.

The mine fire in the 90s caused the shutdown of Sage Mountain which had started as a coal town in the early 1900s and remained our sole industry. Prior to that, the town was alive with miners and the blaring of train horns. My grandparents had moved there in the forties when they were first wed. My grandfather initially started working for the railroad, but the coal industry brought him on at a much higher wage. The labor was demanding and filthy, and my grandparents had always pushed my father to pursue his genuine passion beyond the mines.

In his youth, my father went to play with a classmate over a weekend, and that's when he first experienced skiing. A Norwegian instructor taught lessons, and my grandparents complied. My father took every chance to ski from then on until he was drafted into the military. But fate had other ideas, and after basic training, the right person saw his name and assigned him to be a ski instructor for the military recreation camp. It was more than fate; it was my father's destiny to ski. And he did, soon after reaching the peak where he was the instructor for the US Ski team. From there, he won championships in downhill racing, and he had the fame and glory of a prime athlete of his day when he won the Gold Medal in the Olympics.

This was all before he met my mother, who had been decades his junior, and I came very late in his life— just the one child, which my therapist would point out that it made me put more undue pressure on myself for success, but I felt less. I knew if I had an ultra-successful sibling, I'd feel even worse about my stagnant course.

Having surpassed my thirtieth birthday, work troubles, and being single again, I felt overwhelmed. The year before at the same time, before Theo dumped me, I had hoped by my next birthday that I'd be married, or, at the very least, have a ring on my finger. Instead, I found myself back to square one with the dreaded soon-to-be realities of starting over in the dating world, sprinkled with the loneliness of the impending winter season without a plus one. But just the thought of that made my stomach churn. I had already met the perfect guy, or so I thought. Theo was handsome and athletic… And the exact guy I wanted my father to see me with. I stopped myself with the thought, *Wait a minute. Did I really just think that?*

The revelation of my subconscious sent me down a spiral for the rest of the evening. Had I even liked Theo? Sure, he was astonishingly good-looking… much more so compared to realistic standards. I felt like the lucky one when we were out in public. But he knew it, too. He'd spend hours at the gym lifting weights in front of a mirror. He'd wear clothing that was just a little *too* fitted, and I'd often joke he was the inventor of the selfie. His cologne was overpowering, and I despised its scent. But I was always very complimentary to Theo because that was his love language. In retrospect, I assumed that's why we made it as long as we did. I was very communicative. I told people how much I adored them— the things that made them special— and I expected nothing in return, which was a good thing, because Theo was a man of few words.

I thought back to how we met: at a ribbon cutting for the newest bubble lift at the ski resort. They asked my father to cut the ribbon, which pleased me to no end that he continued to get recognition for his Olympian status. Part of me thought that's why the firm chose me to help design the airport– so they could then use my dad for promotional needs. I was far from being the top designer at the firm, but I was the only one who was local to the area and had a famous skier for a father. Sigh. I thought back to the ribbon cutting, replaying the scene in my mind for the one hundredth time that month.

Theo had attended, hoping to meet my dad, and afterward when my parents and I were trying to settle on a place for lunch, Theo came stumbling over and interrupted our conversation. My father, who always had enough time to meet a fan, shook his hand and let Theo pour it on thick. "My first memory was watching you at the National Championship in 1999. When you tore it up against those young kids– wow. I knew then that I wanted to focus my efforts on skiing as a sport that I could really do for life."

My father appeared deeply touched by that man's words, and I took it as a green light to introduce myself. As Theo lingered, and I had hearts in my eyes, my mother suggested Theo join us for lunch, and the rest was history, or it would've been, had he not dumped me fourteen months later.

My mother didn't ski, and my father loved her. I thought of the definition of love; does it have the bounds of hobbies? If two people don't share every interest or passion, are they incompatible? So, if I wasn't sure that I even liked Theo… If I was pretty sure he was unavailable and only with me out of convenience to get to my father… Did I genuinely love Theo? If I took away his looks, his charm, and the idea of him, what remained? Was any part of our lives ever truly entwined that would make his absence this painful?

I shook the thought from my mind and laughed. The small release of emotion triggered a hysteric fit of humor over Theo's behavior that I never understood, like how he changed his name from Thomas to Theo because he thought it sounded more attractive. Or how he could chat with my father or his friends for hours on end about his ski-jumping, but the moment I wanted to share something close to my heart, it seemed unimportant to him. My sense of humor disappeared, and I realized the darkness of the past several months. The last year of my life was dedicated to the effort of *proving* I was the perfect woman to a man I wasn't even sure I liked, let alone *loved.* These revelations were earth shattering as I rejoiced to God for not answering the very prayers I'd been pleading for that entire time. Theo was *not* the one for me!

As I took a deep breath, I understood it was actually completely over. I could wear my comfortable sweatpants on the weekends without worrying that he might stop by. I could go a day without makeup, styled hair, or fancy clothes. Food was no longer off limits. While I wasn't planning on giving up or letting myself go, I could finally *breathe.*

After a hot shower, a little self-care in the way of a face mask, peppermint tea, and my softest pajamas, I curled up on the couch with my hair still up in a towel. Yes… I felt relieved to be away from Theo. Anything I thought I felt for him was my imagination. After much reflection, I saw that I actually settled with Theo because I thought he was what my father wanted for my life.

What a revelation that was. I thought about my therapist, Anna, and just how right she'd been that whole time; how she had asked me where my need to appease my father came from. As I sorted through my feelings in silence, I prayed that I could let that desire go. Despite the crucial importance of maintaining a close bond with my life-giving parents, I no longer wanted to make life-altering decisions based on perceived notions of their desires for me. And Anna was right about my skirting the blame in situations. I'd been so hurt at Theo for not wanting a relationship that I had been tiptoeing around that entire time… I wasn't even behaving like myself. If I hadn't encouraged our relationship as hard as I did, would we ever have even started one? I doubted it.

> *Dear Lord, Please direct my path. I'm surrendering the sense of control I desperately want to cling to, but I can't anymore. Only You know the plan You have for my life, and I trust You, Lord. Amen.*

From then on, I decided to forge my own path in life and love while giving God full control. When I was ready, I would look for the partner that God had planned for me, not who I thought my father would want as a son-in-law.

My father… I needed to call him soon. I got up from the couch and moved to where his poster from his cover of the box of Wheaties hung up in my living room; the one he had just razzed me about being the focal point of my living room. I thought about what he said, but I had always kept it hanging up in my bedroom when I was young, so when my grandmother left me her condo in her will, it just seemed natural to have it on my main wall. I looked over at him, realizing that despite my personal breakthrough in the wrong relationship I had just gotten out of, I was still not ready to tell my dad what had transpired. He had just been so successful that I felt like a dud, stunted in my growth compared to his long list of accomplishments. Oh well, I thought. Those feelings weren't real nor were they valid.

My phone dinged and pulled me out of my daydream. I reached for it in my pajama pocket and saw a text from the youth group leader, Mickey, at Sage Creek Church, reminding me of my night to bring the treats.

> **Hello, Claire! I'm sending you a short list of what to bring for Float Night tomorrow. You'll need to go to Baxter's store in order to find the Dairy-Free for Coleen. Let me know the total, and we will Venmo you. Thx!**
>
> **(typing..)**
>
> **(typing..)**

2-Liter of Root Beer

2-Liter of Orange Soda

2-Liter of Sprite

Ice Creams:

Rainbow Sherbet

Strawberry

Vanilla

Dairy-Free Vanilla

As I skimmed over the list, the distraction it brought pleased me. Nothing made me happier than working with teenagers. According to them, I was cool because I hadn't conformed to the lifestyle around there— a backwards way of looking at the fact I didn't ski, but I thought, *I'll take it.*

I had little involvement at the youth group other than serving as a glorified errands gal those days. But when Mickey had asked me to help last year, it had been out of the blue and yet just what I needed. Spending time with the youth in my community at that level was fulfilling. And at that time, it provided a much-needed mental escape from the recent devastation in my life.

Chapter 4

December 23rd

"Thank you, Claire, for your work on the new airport plan. We've got everything set in motion now." Patricia's words were blunt. I was holding my breath, assuming her reason for calling me first thing that morning was to fire me. But she surprised me.

"The CEO was happy with the finishing touches on your design, such as the stone fireplaces in the cozy seating areas, and he wants you to explore the idea of designing an outdoor patio— something that will still be in a secured area for flyers to use after going through security. It's a newer concept that his team would like to get a feel for. Of course, if you think this is too much right now considering everything else you have going on… And with it being December 23rd…," she trailed off.

"No! I mean, it isn't too much. I'd love nothing more than to work on this. Please send me the details and requirements, and I'll get to it immediately."

With my parents being out of town for the holidays in Alaska, and since they assumed I'd be with Theo, I had nothing on the docket whatsoever. I was grateful for the distraction. I did nothing for Christmas that year— didn't even put up a tree. Why wouldn't I work instead?

Hanging up the phone, I knew Patricia didn't like me very much. Truthfully, I didn't care for her either, but her being so cordial on the phone proved she was patted on the back by the higher ups, thanks to me. She was a high-powered businesswoman, and I knew I shouldn't have missed so many days, but it was clear from the start that she didn't care for me. It didn't matter, though— not then, anyway. The relief spurred through my bones, and I felt like I could do cartwheels through my living room. I turned the volume up on my computer, so I could hear new emails arriving as I waited for the plans. I would turn that over as timely as possible to help secure my job, at least as long as I could.

The email from Patricia came seven minutes later, while I was pouring myself another cup of coffee from my worn French press, the same one I'd used since college. As I squeezed the last of its contents into my cup, I topped it off with a little cream from a handheld frother and raced back to my computer. It was time to get to work.

Patricia's message was curt and to the point. "Here are the blueprints. Let's see what you can do."

That was it— no signature or anything. Though I hadn't cared about anything but my heartbreak when I had gotten myself on that thin ice, since I was dealing with the repercussions, the situation became all but *threatening*. But I could do it. It would be fine. I opened the blueprints and figured out the space's ebb and flow, which wasn't clear at first, but once I understood that, designing would be a breeze.

My process for designing was immersive. If possible, I wanted to be at the site in question, and that would normally mean I needed to make a quick trip out to the airport to see where that space would go. But I was short on time. I needed to do it entirely from memory. I closed my eyes and remembered the town that used to be where the giant airport currently was before the wrecking ball had come through and torn it down in favor of a shiny new town owned by the ski resort.

"If the space is to the west of the runway, that means it faces Superstition Run, which means… It used to be where Jack's Ice Cream Parlor was." I pictured the mountain view that the outdoor space would have from every season. My memories rushed back to a time when my parents took me out to get ice cream. The flavor of the season was peppermint, and the tiny flecks of candy canes stuck to my teeth. I snapped back to the task at hand, but it gave me an idea.

Eight hours later, I sent the finished proof over to Patricia for her initial review. I mumbled a small prayer as I put my head over my hands. After spending a long, grueling day glued to my computer, I felt a surge of elation at having something to show, even if it was only for a moment. However, since it was only Tuesday, there remained ample time in my work week for the possibility of getting fired. I glanced one more time at the rendition I had made, and it pleased me.

The theme for the space was Après-ski. It had floor to ceiling glass walls with outdoor heaters spread throughout, so patrons could enjoy it in the deepest winter freeze. A unique bar made from vintage skis was the centerpiece of the space, and they would specialize in peppermint drinks. Three leather sectional couches graced the floor plan, with a separate section for smoking cigars along with an industrial ventilation system, making it safe for all patrons. Glass orb lights hung from the metal ceiling and, just for fun, a portrait of my dad bombing a downhill race on the wall. Patricia had a 3D mockup of this to tour, and I loved it. Whether she did was out of my hands. Just then, my phone dinged with the reminder I set about supplies for the youth group.

*****

"Did you find everything we needed?" Mickey jumped up to help me when I walked through the door, carrying all six bags in my arms.

"Yes, I sure did. I even improvised a bit." An awkward smile crossed my lips as he discovered a pint of peppermint ice cream in the last bag. "What can I say? It's my favorite."

Mickey shivered and shrugged, sticking his tongue out. "Sure, but with soda!? Yuck, Claire!"

Mickey loved to tease, but he was right. I hadn't thought about what soda that would pair with. "I guess I better just eat it out of the container, then." With a sigh, I grabbed a spoon as the teens filed in.

Mickey greeted everyone with a high five, and then the kids came over to fist bump me. I was told it was as good as shaking hands those days.

"Okay, guys. We have a few fun activities for tonight, including a talk on our favorite subject. Anyone wanna guess what that is?"

Mickey was so vibrant and engaging, I almost wanted to take a stab at it but left it to the teens.

Melody spoke up. "Peer pressure?"

Mickey clapped. "Good idea, Melody! I had nothing in mind to talk about tonight, so that should do fine."

Laughing it off, a few of the kids groaned dramatically, but I knew they loved Mickey, and everything he talked about was always spot on.

"But first, we have something exciting that we need to discuss, gang."

My ears perked up as I started sorting out the Solo cups for the ice cream floats. I did not know what Mickey was referring to.

"Thanks to a *very* generous donation from Brian's parents to our group bonding fund," Mickey ran over and gave him a fist bump, "and a matching grant from our community ski resort, we can take a four-night ski vacation right here at Sage Mountain, starting on December 28th. One of the new luxury lodges will accommodate us, all our meals are included, and most importantly, our group will have four ski instructors assigned to us. They will base the ski instructors on ability, so for all my pros out there, don't worry. So? Who's with me?"

Mickey singled me out, fully knowing my history with the sport. My jaw dropped while our group of teens cheered. "I have already spoken to your parents, but I made them promise to let me tell you," Mickey said. "Several of them will be with us as chaperones, so don't get too excited. Except I am because most of your parents are totally dope. Except yours, Rachel. Your dad gave me that speeding ticket last year and… Well, don't worry, we're cool now, and he's coming too. Everyone is welcome!"

Mickey shot me a glance and smiled eagerly.

God sure has a sense of humor. At first, I felt dread looming over me or the schematics of how I could make it happen. I marveled at the miraculous situation He had placed me in. The question was not whether I wanted to go, but how could I make it happen? To be honest, I wasn't sure what Patricia would do if I asked for my remaining day. I bowed my head and said a prayer over it. No matter what, I would be there with the group in the off hours. I considered a scenario where I took my computer with me and set up an office. And then to heck with it; I'd take that Friday off so at least I had an extra day on the slopes. That thought triggered the onset of real panic. Taking my last vacation day to take part in something out of my comfort zone was not exactly what I had in mind, but there I was, letting God lead me.

The revelation of my prayers coming into fruition made me tear up. God was giving me an opportunity, steering me towards a goal of mine that I could either meet or miss, but either way, I was going to take the chance. *Thank you, Lord.*

I couldn't focus on the rest of the night because of the realization that I would not only be on skis in a week's time, but that my lessons and hotel stay would be covered. God had blessed me tenfold. After a successful float night and an impactful sermon from Mickey, the kids filtered out, and I stayed behind to pepper Mickey with questions.

"What in the world, Mickey?" My eyes were as wide as my smile.

"It would be great if you could join us however long you're able to. I know your schedule is busy with work, but you can just come and go as you please. It's all covered. We won't be doing much in the evenings together, thanks to the multitude of parents attending. That's off our plate. Think of it as a brief vacation before it gets too busy around here that we won't even be able to see straight." He gave me a partial hug as his phone buzzed.

A brief vacation? That was two suggestions in one week. God sure had a way of surprising me.

"Okay, the 'Mrs.' needs me back home. Her feet hurt, and she has a late-night craving for beignets." Mickey put his hands in a prayer position. "Lord, please let something still be open for my pregnant wife, or she will make me sleep on the couch again."

I laughed at Mickey and told him where he could find the beignets. "And don't worry, I'll be skiing. I was planning on taking lessons this season anyway… It's something I've been thinking about. This is all an answer to my prayers, really, especially as a distraction from everything else going on."

Mickey knew about Theo breaking up with me, but he didn't seem too bothered. He never liked Theo, and he made that fact known.

"So, I just wanted to say thank you for inviting me along. The only thing is my work schedule. I will be there with bells on, but I'll be tied up from 9 to 5…"

Mickey put his hand to his chest, and at first, I assumed it was sarcastically. We had a very playful relationship, since I'd known him for most of my life after meeting him in kindergarten. He was like a brother to me and the reason I found out about the needs of the youth group.

"I'm touched by that, Claire. And I want to hear all about it and your work schedule once the dragon is fed—Tamara, I mean. I love that woman to the ends of the earth, but boy does she have a fragile temper right now. I better get going… Pray for me that her third trimester is easier on all of us, okay?"

He waved and shut the door behind him. Once I finished bagging up the last of the trash, I grabbed what remained of my peppermint pint of ice cream out of the freezer, hit the lights, and locked up behind me.

When I got home, I scoured my closet and dresser for skiing attire. I had white snow pants, a red jacket, and a thick white turtleneck— sure, a little 80s maybe, but it would work. I put the outfit on to see how it fit and was pleased it all felt great on and even looked flattering. I stood in my closet in front of the mirror. The red jacket brought out a warm hue in my strawberry blonde hair and made my blue eyes look a little brighter. I liked the jacket, and when I bought it at the end of last season on sale, I had pictured Theo proposing to me in it. I knew that sounded pathetic, but it was my dream to be married to him and have the picture-perfect husband. All I could do in that relationship was try to show him I could be his picture-perfect wife, except for the skiing part. That just seemed so far out of reach.

I silently thanked the Lord for not answering that prayer for me since I had realized there wasn't much to that relationship. It still didn't help the disappointment of starting over.

As I went to change into some comfortable pajamas, I hung my ski clothes up on a hanger together and placed them on the doorknob of my closet. I wanted to see that outfit for the rest of the week as I prepared myself for my second chance at skiing.

December 26th

The rest of my work week involved much back and forth with Patricia. She didn't like my design at first, but then again, she wasn't the one who needed to. It all came down to the team of James Walker. Polishing things as much as possible was crucial, so I made some adjustments. We spent time on the phone and several hours on a video call where we both made suggestions to the base of the design. I felt like our relationship was strengthening, and I appreciated it.

Thursday afternoon, Patricia sent the finished design off to her bosses. It included a champagne and cigar bar, custom ski furniture and two large faux-antler chandeliers because no animal in nature could have produced something to the scale we needed. The plan was fresh and unique, and Patricia's voice exuded excitement as she bid me a good night. I closed the applications on my computer and powered it off.

"Lord, thank you for turning this week around. I didn't know that it could be turned around, but you are the God of miracles, after all."

After scouring my drawer of takeout menus, I decided it wouldn't hurt to mix things up that night and go out to eat instead of ordering in. The confidence in Patricia's voice had been contagious, and my crushed feelings for Theo were fading. I applied mascara, some rosy blush, and a pink lip gloss. My strawberry blonde hair hung straight, so I zapped my roots with a little hairspray to give it some lift. Slipping into dark jeans and a black mock neck top that hugged my figure, I pulled my red ski jacket off its hanger. That night, I wanted to at least look the part of a Sage Mountain skiing woman, and once I put on my warm and fuzzy snow boots, I felt like one, too.

The Barn Door Bar & Grill was three blocks from my condo and about all I could muster in that cold. I'd forgotten just how frigid the day's forecast was. It had been a brutal winter that far, having only just begun, and the forecast was calling for record snowfall. I pulled the black hat out of my jacket pocket and pulled it tight around my ears. The faux fur pom on top of my hat bounced as I walked, making me feel self-conscious, but as I looked around, I seamlessly blended in with the mix of people who were out.

"How many?" the host Tina asked as she looked behind me, expecting to see the gorgeous Theo, no doubt. I shook my head.

"Just me tonight. I'll take a seat at the bar." I couldn't handle taking up an entire booth for myself, or worse, getting a round table in the middle of the place like I had at the piano bar on my birthday. *No, better not risk that again.* However, as far as I knew, they didn't play any musical instruments at that bar. As I fluidly walked to the row of bar stools, the one I had been walking toward was between two that were empty. Suddenly, a group came from the left and took them. I stopped in my tracks. Reversing my course, I went to the left of two empty stools when a woman absentmindedly placed her purse on one, not seeing me behind her. It was down to one bar stool, so I grabbed it with both hands and slid onto it.

"What can I get you to drink?" The woman behind the bar had jet black hair with thick bangs that looked like they tickled her long eyelashes.

I mumbled for a moment like I'd never consumed liquids in my entire life before stammering out something about hot tea.

"Coming right up. I'll bring you a menu, too."

I let out a sigh of relief that the food was near as I scoped out my surroundings. The place was packed for a Thursday night, but the couple next to me was mumbling about a big snow that night and creating excitement for a Friday powder day, which they claimed was better than Christmas.

I felt the man on the other side of me rotate his bar stool back and face forward. "Can I get a Pepsi?" he asked the bartender. His voice was deep and raspy. I didn't want to look over, since doing so would almost guarantee an awkward greeting with us sitting so closely together, but suddenly I didn't have a choice.

"Hey."

He was now speaking to me, so I looked in his direction and gave an obligatory hello. He was a scruffy, dark-haired guy with thick, black-rimmed glasses. He was also wearing a platinum wedding band on his left ring finger, which solidified his introduction just being one of friendship.

Not a moment later, the wife in question came around the corner. A beautiful blonde, she wore a black sweater dress, black hosiery, and furry boots. She took the seat on the opposite side of him.

The bartender returned with my drink. "Here you go: peppermint tea. Our special tonight is the steak, but I'll let you in on a secret: We use the same tender steak on our sandwich and salad."

She was speaking my language. I ordered the steak salad with a side of curly fries and turned my head to see what was happening behind me.

Everyone glued their faces to the outside window as fat, round snowflakes fell. It was enchanting, and the excitement was electric. I had to admit that it made me feel a little giddy, too. The new opportunity for me to learn to ski was bringing out a child-like enchantment inside of me, while most importantly, making me look at this powdery ground covering that made it impossible to drive for five months out of the year with a better lens: one of excitement.

After a delicious meal, I paid my check and started towards the door, taking my bright red coat off the rack and sliding into my hat and gloves while using a bench to tighten up the laces on my snow boots. When I looked up, my eyes met those of a very handsome stranger which caught me off guard and caused me to slide right into a wet puddle left from another patron's snowy shoes. I couldn't tell you how long I was airborne, or the noise I made while my legs flew up from under me and catapulted me backwards. All I knew was I garnered the attention of the entire bar and stole the show. So much for blending in.

While I lay on the cold, dark tile of the upscale bar, I thought if I my sprawled body just stayed still, it would all go away. They would return to business as usual and just work around me until it was time to close, at which time I could then slip out the back door and no one would think another thought. I quickly learned that couldn't be possible when a woman screamed. It was a little overdramatic, so I was sure I would be missing a leg or an arm when I got up. The sounds of the clunky boots shuffling around me made my head rattle. I had accidentally caused a slip-n-fall lawsuit.

I sat up as I slowly opened my eyes. A hand was out in front of me, and I accepted it, and when I stood, I was face to face with that handsome man. I let out a gasp as I realized it was the man from the piano bar.

"Miss… Are you okay?" Tina, the hostess, pulled out a flashlight normally used to check IDs and pointed it in my unprepared eyes. I snapped them back shut, almost falling again from the sheer embarrassment of it all. I gave the hostess points for not adding insult to injury by calling me *ma'am.*

"Yes, I'm fine… just a little embarrassed is all." I made my best effort at laughing it off, realizing only then was I still holding the man's hand. So, I did what anyone would do in that situation. I gave it a shake and introduced myself before I let it go. "Thank you for helping me. Claire Riley."

His face lit up like the twinkling lights hanging in a snowflake pattern in the corner of the bar. "Nice to meet you, Claire. I'm Blake."

I wondered if he remembered me from a few weeks back at the piano bar, but before I could say anything, the bartender suddenly appeared beside us and leaned in and linked arms with Blake. Tina and I both sighed in unison as it was clear that man was taken.

"And I was just leaving," I replied.

I told Tina goodnight, and she waved at me, giving me a silly face while pointing at the happy couple, who were now immersed in conversation. But at the last moment, I saw Blake look over his shoulder at me and smile.

The snowy walk home almost made me forget about the bitter chill that made my face numb and my ears hurt, despite wearing a heavy hat. I sighed, thinking about the handsome hunk I had just met for the second time this month. Though I may have been in a rough patch of life, there was something about that taken man that gave me hope for the future. Everything would work out to God's plan, and in my heart, I felt I would find love… eventually, anyway. *Tomorrow is a new day*, I thought. *You never know what a new day will bring.*

Chapter 5

December 27th

It turned out the new day brought destruction to my life. I awoke to a tsunami of notifications on my design software that certain aspects had been "red-flagged" by another user, meaning they would need to be removed from the design. Once I saw just how many there were, I quickly realized that Patricia had personally rejected my design— the one she was happy with the night before. The sound of the fracturing proverbial ice around me was just too much to handle. I knew this was it for my job, and instead of waiting in a torturous state of limbo for Patricia to call, I called her.

"Claire," her breathy tone sounded like she was half asleep, or upset. I suspected it wasn't the latter but couldn't imagine the former either. "It's a no on the Après cigar bar. I can't see how it would work… It's just too *cliché.* Anyway, my tail was really on the line here. Claire, I'm going to have to let you go. You just don't have the vision to pull this off."

Her words stung, but another strange phenomenon happened similar to the emotions I was working through after Theo dumped me: I felt relief. Yes, I was scared out of my mind for my food, healthcare, and financial security. Yet, all I could think about was that I could now take part in the ski retreat that started the next day.

I thanked Patricia for the opportunities she lent to me, the experience I gained, and I stated all of those lovely platitudes that people say when they've just gotten fired, but I couldn't get off the phone fast enough. She had some offers about Human Resources being in touch with my severance package, which was a little bonus I wasn't expecting. It might have even helped float my property tax bill for another month. When I finally got off the call, I took a long, hot shower and robotically packed my suitcase for the retreat.

December 28th

The next morning came, and I sent my parents a message telling them that I would be away at a church retreat for the rest of the week, purposely omitting the part about it being a ski retreat right there in Sage Mountain. Though there was cell phone service at the lodge, I wasn't ready to face the music with my double whammy of getting dumped and fired in the same period. I cringed when I remembered that my father would have the airport dedication and ribbon cutting ceremony to hold when it opened in a few short months. He would know either way that I no longer worked for the firm, but I decided to cross that bridge when I got there. A moment later, my mother sent me a thumbs-up emoji and asked me to tell her everything when I got home.

After I dressed, I wasn't sure I felt as good in the outfit as I did when I tried it on a few days before. Between the ice cream and my emotional snacking, it was apparent I'd packed on a few extra pounds overnight, making my waistline a little uncomfortable. After some scientific testing, though, I realized the button on my pants was secure and held no risk of popping. The back seam was strong and most likely wouldn't split. The only thing I had to worry about was the loud *swishing* sound as my thighs boldly announced to the world I was in motion. Sighing, I checked the minor mascara I added to my otherwise invisible lashes. It was a little too cold and dry out to wear eye makeup, but flaking off was a risk I would take.

The drive to the new lodge was gorgeous. I had been all over Sage Mountain on the ground level, and while it was safe to say that I'd seen every nook and cranny of that place without skiing, I hadn't explored the mountains very much. The new resort was built into a rolling hillside, and according to its brochure, was ski-in/ski-out with its own chair lift systems. Given the rapid growth there, it wasn't surprising that I didn't know this. It was easy to lose track of every new hotel. I was eager to see it.

I arrived at the Superstition Peak Lodge half an hour before the rest of the group, so I could get my bearings for the lodging situation. I assumed that I would bunk with half of the girls, but it turned out the resort had separate rooms set aside for the adults, and I would share a room with Joy, Katrina's mom. At the very last minute while I was walking up to the concierge counter, Joy texted me that she bunked in the same room with her daughter, so I was completely off the hook for any chaperone duties. She had invited me to their room to watch movies, as they were bringing a pre-loaded HDMI stick with several chick flicks on it, but I wasn't ready to commit to anything yet.

The concierge was an outgoing, thirty-something man. He had a brisk accent that sounded east coast. "I'm Zeek. Let's give you a quick run-down of where everything is, shall we?"

I agreed and appreciated it since the layout was confusing to navigate, even as he took me on the tour. The lodge was much bigger than I realized with over 300 rooms, which blew me away. He eagerly chatted to me about the expectations they had for the upcoming season. Once I set my bags in my room, he showed me to the ski room.

"The lodge is three buildings, and they connect via a sky bridge. Here, we will take an elevator to the bridge level where we can enter Building 2 where our ski outfitter is."

We finally made it to the ski gear area.

"Here we are. We have your group scheduled to meet the instructors each morning at 9:30, except for today where we have you down for a half day starting at noon. You'll want to come in here and get fitted for boots as soon as everyone gets here, so we can get those assigned with gear. And from here, we will just go down this walkway."

I followed him down a hallway to an outdoor area with a metal grate covering the ground to catch the wet snow. The icy chill caught my nose with a familiar surprise.

"And there's the bunny hill. You'll all meet here every morning."

For the term *bunny hill*, I always expected much less incline, but this was the one place I had an experience with.

"Let me know if there's anything we can help your group with during your stay. Enjoy."

The concierge returned inside, holding the door for me behind him.

"I suppose you could walk me back to the other building so I can find it again," I smiled sheepishly, and he laughed, waving me over, and we walked back.

"Any plans for New Year's Eve?"

His question caught me off guard. Was he asking me out? My social skills hadn't taken that much of a hit that I didn't even know what was happening… right? Then again, I thought I was getting engaged when I got dumped instead. "I haven't thought that far ahead. Is there anything fun going on?" I gave him a once-over to really *see* the man I was speaking to. He was rather attractive; that was clear with his jet-black hair and blueish gray eyes. There was an evolving tone to his voice that I couldn't place, but almost everyone living and working in Sage Mountain was from elsewhere, so that didn't even phase me anymore.

"Depends on where you look." He winked at me, making my cheeks betray me instantly.

I internally screamed at my blushing, which always betrayed me. First thing after New Year's, I vowed to call a doctor about my cheeks reddening at every drop of a pin. I did not know what he meant by that, but I didn't have to wonder long as we stepped back into the elevator. He looked around, as if someone could hear him, while we were alone.

"My buddies and I started a little bit of an underground thing. Do you like club music?" He was grinning ear to ear, eagerly anticipating my answer, but my facial expression must have said it all.

I wanted to say "yes," but it wasn't the truth. Still, it was hard. "I do… not." There was nothing I disliked more than loud booming beats and flashing lights. "I'm afraid that sort of thing triggers my migraines." He looked away in defeat. "But I wish you much success."

Every relationship had deal breakers, and partying was the biggest one for me. I just *didn't* party. My idea of having a great time was getting up early and watching the sunrise. The elevator doors opened, and Zeek bolted out without another word. *Oh well*, I thought. Instead of going to my room, I loitered in the lobby while I waited for the youth group.

Exploring the area, I turned into a lounge that was so stunning, it took my breath away. The ceilings were impossibly tall, showing an intricate beam pattern that must have taken months to design and complete. Extending to the ceiling, the tan stone fireplace had sparkling glass pieces in the fire, glistening elegantly. The windows overlooked bright, red gondolas and the "V," just like at my condo, but much closer. The space was enchanting.

There was a full-scale bar with several seating areas, but a small sign on the bar top said they weren't open until the evening. It explained their offerings of self-serve hot drinks on a nearby adjacent table. The selection looked divine; they had three large vats of liquids: hot chocolate, coffee, and decaf. Next to them, they had shiny glass jars filled to the top with fluffy marshmallows, sprinkles, and cinnamon candies. A pastry bottle of fresh whipped cream sat in the center in a small bucket with ice.

Checking my watch, I went for it. I was officially on vacation and considering I was now unemployed, I thought I had better make this last hurrah count. I didn't know when, if *ever*, I would go on another trip. Ten in the morning was the perfect time to make myself a tall drink with extra whipped cream and marshmallows. I was sprinkling on the cinnamon when Mickey tapped me on the shoulder.

"Morning, Claire. You want to do me a solid and make Tamara one of those while I check in? She's got low blood sugar this morning and trust me when I say it would be for the good of the world to fix that."

I looked at Tamara who was standing right next to Mickey.

"Ignore him, Claire. So nice to see you." She leaned in and gave me a hug, her beautiful, golden-brown curls cascading over her shoulders.

"Tamara, you look cuter every moment. Would you like a hot chocolate? It's frigid outside, and you have the best excuse in the world, as you're drinking for two."

Mickey snorted and patted her perfectly round baby bump, before walking over to the front desk.

"All jokes, you two! Yes, Claire, I would love one."

I handed her my first creation while I made a second with even more marshmallows that time and joined her on the leather sectional in front of the grand fireplace.

"Mickey said you're taking ski lessons, too. I think that's wonderful. If I could, I would, but I'm fearful of falling or worse, falling asleep. I've been so tired these days, and I'm nowhere near the finish line."

I looked at Mickey's stunning wife whom he started dating in high school. It was never a question for either of them. They were destined to be together and didn't have to wonder when or if they would marry.

"Yes. When in Rome… Any baby names picked out?" I quickly changed the subject; it was refreshing to talk about something else for a change other than myself, skiing, and how the two things did not mix well.

"We like Henry for a boy and— "

"Elsie for a girl," Mickey interjected, appearing behind Tamara with room keys in both hands. He kissed her on the top of her head before sorting out the keys. The teens started arriving, and Mickey went to greet them.

"I'm so happy for you, Tamara. Really, what a magical time this is— the beginning of your beautiful family."

Tamara smiled and patted her baby bump. "It will happen for you, too, Claire. I feel it in my bones."

She stood up, taking my hand in hers for a moment and then went to join Mickey and the teens. I sat there for a minute longer, taking in the unexpected words of encouragement. Saying a silent prayer, I felt the words she said and told the Lord I would love nothing more than for them to become my reality.

Once everyone got settled in, it was time for our first ski lesson of the week. Just as Mickey said, we divided the groups into beginner, moderate, and advanced skiers. Surprisingly, most of the kids were in the beginner category. Though they were half my age, there was a redeeming quality about that for my own mental health.

Once everyone was dressed in ski gear, helmets, boots, and poles, our instructors had our skis waiting for us outside the door. Before we went out, Mickey pulled out a list and named off who would ski with each instructor. My group was last, so I took the chance to apply sunscreen on my face before departing.

My group was made up of myself and seven teens. We got paired with Tara, a lovely twenty-something blonde with hot pink ski pants. The uniform jacket was a long parka in a brilliant red, similar to my jacket but longer, and it had a giant Sage Mountain logo on the back. She looked like a walking Valentine. It worked for her. She was friendly, quickly introducing herself to me with a handshake before greeting the teens.

"Alright, gang. This is going to be fun! First, we are going to start with an assessment to see ability. Raise your hand if you've skied before."

Most of the group did, except for two.

"Great. Alright, you two, you stay with me. Everyone else, if you're comfortable with it, I'd like you to go up the magic carpet and ski down, one by one, so I can see what you need to work on."

The adrenaline shot through my veins as I somehow got roped into going first. "I can't, I'm shy," I joked with one teen, Gracie, who stood her ground and insisted I go first. "Okay, I'll go."

As I stepped onto the magic carpet, memories of the times I had been there flooded my mind. Over the years, I'd made several attempts to take up skiing but never took it seriously and gave up when I didn't immediately become a pro. Good skiers made it look so easy, but in reality, it was a sport that required practice and skill. And for the first time in my life, I was taking lessons from an instructor. As I reached the top of the bunny hill, I looked down to Tara who was smiling and waiting for me to come down, so I tried my best to do that smoothly.

The wind picked up, swirling a fresh powder of snow around me and simulating the feeling of going faster than I was. I knew from my dad that the goal was to keep my skis parallel to each other, but I tried that too quickly and fell face down in the snow.

"It's okay, Claire. Keep going!" Tara called out.

Keep going? I was covered in snow. My mission failed. I was remembering why I hated skiing so much while I pushed my upper body up. As I sat in the snow and unclipped my skis with a pole so I could walk out of that situation, someone else came up beside me.

"Take my hand."

A black glove appeared in front of me, and I did. After he helped me up, I looked at his face, but between his black helmet, metallic goggles, and neck gaiter, I could not see who the man was or what he looked like. He set my skis down in front of him to clip back into.

"There, you're all set."

That was it, and he skied off before I could thank him. Although my ego was bruised, I felt fine otherwise, so I shrugged it off and, with Tara's encouragement, I clipped back into the skis and tried my best to follow through. When I made it back to her, she gave me a pat on the back.

"Great job, Claire. Falling is inevitable, but getting back up and trying again is where the commitment lies within us. You got this, Claire."

I did not feel the same sentiment… In fact, I felt the furthest from it.

When the last teen returned from their assessment, Tara told us we all had varying abilities, and she asked if everyone wanted to start from scratch. We were in overwhelming agreement with that idea.

"Fantastic. Now, let's begin by starting our lesson in ski positions. Everybody watch me and do as I do, okay?"

She put her skis out parallel in front of her, and we all followed suit. Thankfully, I was already standing that way, if not just a little more pigeon-toed.

"This is called 'French Fries.' This is how we ski when we want to glide. Got it? Now for the next."

She put her ski tips closer together, making a triangle.

"This is called 'Pizza.' This is what we do when we want to turn, to slow down, or to even stop before we learn how to properly do that. Claire, be careful with this as it's brutal on the knees past age twenty-five."

She giggled, and I thanked her for the warning.

"Now, let's put these two positions into play. Everyone, let's hop on the magic carpet to take us to the top of the bunny hill!"

Despite my second time on it in fifteen minutes, and it only moving at three mph, I wasn't expecting the magic carpet to almost trip me when I stepped on. My body was working so hard to glide over like I had any sense on skis at all, but the carpet was moving slower than I was by the time I made it, causing me to lean forward and nearly take out all of my teens like a row of dominoes. Thankfully, my ski poles caught me.

The way down the hill that time was different as the focus wasn't on me, but rather relaxed as I was casually trying the different stances. It brought back many memories of the last time I tried to ski, which was well over a decade ago. My dad, Mac, had been invited to Palisades Tahoe for a "Legends of the West" race, and he took me along. We had four days to roam around, and my mother and I decided we would go sledding. But when she twisted her ankle on ice the night before, I decided to rent some equipment for the day. I quickly felt frustrated, clumsy, and far too cold. It was a miserable time trying to make my body move like an expert, though I was starting from square one. I thought I gave it up for good after that.

I was seeing a pattern. Every time in my life that I'd faced a challenge, I'd given up. How would things be different if, instead of giving up, I'd faced the difficulties head on? Sighing, I realized I was once again having a pity party. No one had made me come. No one had forced me to take that lesson, and in fact, I had made that choice myself. It was something I'd always aspired to do, and yet, I'd never followed through on. When would I ever learn to take responsibility for my choices? I said a silent prayer.

> *Lord, please free me from my own mind. I accept the responsibility and consequences of my actions. Let me be patient as You are with me. I thank You for the blessing and answer to my prayers by bringing me here. Lord, let me live without fear and enjoy this experience as much as possible. I want Your will for my life, not my own. In your name, Amen.*

The hour flew by and by the end of the lesson, all the teens were racing down the hill, and I was with them. That time, things felt different. Part of that was due to Tara cheering me on and giving me helpful tips with zero criticism. The other part was admitting I was starting at zero and learning the basics. When all was said and done, I had a good time. Before we went inside, my cheeks hurt. It took a few minutes for me to realize it was from smiling so hard. *Thank you, Lord, for the unexpected.*

"Claire, wait up!" Tara shouted before gracefully gliding over to me on her skis and unclipping them from her boots in a fluid motion. "Great job, today. You have some good movements. I want you to really prepare for when you do a turn; you lift one ski up, ever so slightly."

"Thanks, Tara. I will think about that. Looking forward to our next lesson."

She reached over and opened the door and we both walked inside, taking off our helmets. My teeth were chattering.

"You're welcome. I know it's hard; there's going to be a lot we cram into the week, but I hope you walk away with confidence to practice."

"I'm so glad I did this and that you are my instructor. You have such a gentle way of teaching with no negativity or criticism, and I really appreciate that."

"Aww, you're so welcome. I know what you're saying… know the type all too well. Some people can be quite harsh, taking their frustrations out on others. But for me, my passion in life is skiing, and I want other people to find a way to enjoy it. That's more important than always being perfect."

I agreed with her sentiment as she spoke. "Do you want to get lunch?" I asked her, while skimming the room. All the teens were with family or friends. I was riding solo.

"Oh, I'd love to, but my boyfriend is coming to meet me. He should be here any second."

I realized when she brought him up, that I'd gone one hour without thinking of Theo. Instantly, he was back at the top of my mind. "That's okay. Maybe another day, I'll be here until New Year's."

"Absolutely, Claire. I would love to get to know you more. Now that the ski resort is open, I feel like I see my boyfriend all the time. He likes to spend as much time as he can up here."

"I know the type." *That's just like Theo*, I thought.

"Yeah. I feel the same, mostly, but since I also work here, I enjoy some time away. It's a very new relationship, though. We only just started dating like two weeks ago. He is supposed to be leaving for the entire winter in just a few days. Now, he tells me he's ready to get serious in our relationship. What girl doesn't want to hear that? I mean, he's so, so gorgeous. He's the perfect guy: kind, tall, wants to settle down. I just don't know if it all seems way too fast."

Another employee walked by, and she stopped talking as he smiled and waved at her.

"Is that him?" I whispered, playfully elbowing her in the ribs. "He's totally adorable."

She bit her lip and shook her head. "No."

I could sense some hesitancy in her voice.

"Oh, there's my boyfriend. I better go. I'll see you in a bit, Claire."

She winked at me while pointing to a group of people, and I waved her goodbye. My eyes followed her as she went into the cluster of people in ski gear. I took off my gloves and felt my face. My sunscreen had crusted up in a few spots, so I started towards the restroom when I stopped dead in my tracks. Tara and her boyfriend were walking right towards me. Tara's boyfriend was *Theo*– as in, Theo McCain, who had just dumped me less than three weeks ago on his way to Canada to be repped by SkySki. According to Tara's timeline, they began dating immediately after, and suddenly he was ready to settle down.

Sweat broke out on my hairline. I needed to escape. I was confident that Theo hadn't seen me yet, so I quickly spun around, but found myself awkwardly facing three people who were right in the middle of a conversation that halted the moment I joined them.

"Hey… Hi, umm, I'm sorry to interrupt. Please let me just stand here for a moment because that's my ex-boyfriend with his new girlfriend and…"

I rambled off into silence while two of the men laughed and said it was okay. I looked at the third man in horror. It was the man from the piano bar, because *of course it was*– Blake, the hunk who I also saw Thursday night when he picked me up after I slipped. Apparently, he was making his rounds whenever I was in need. His smile was just as dazzling as I remembered. In his hands he held a blue neck gaiter and metallic goggles. Wait… *He* was the mystery man who'd helped me up on the bunny hill an hour ago? Was he an angel undercover who appeared every time I took a spill? My knees felt so weak with anxiety knowing that Theo was behind me, that I felt like I could topple over just to test the theory.

"Well, if it isn't Claire Riley," Blake announced.

He winked at me as my knees felt an aftershock of embarrassment. His voice had been a touch too loud, and I heard a familiar set of feet clunking up behind me. All of this was just so overwhelming. It was then that I remembered the sunscreen on my face as a piece flaked off and went past my eyes like paper thrown out of a window. I squeezed my eyes shut and regained composure. He had a girlfriend anyway. What was the harm in having a conversation?

"It's Blake, right? From the piano bar and The Barn Door last night…"

"Don't forget the bunny hill," he winked at me.

I felt my knees turn to putty.

"Blake Walker, at your service."

As we conversed, something caught his eye just past me. By the time I realized all three men were looking at someone who'd walked up, it was too late.

"Claire? Is that you?" Theo was speaking to me.

You don't owe him anything, I told myself.

"Claire?"

Theo took me by the shoulder, coaxing me to spin around like a circus poodle, but I didn't budge.

"Yep," I mumbled under my breath, refusing to turn around. I was certain my face was as red as my coat. I couldn't look at Blake or any of the men. For the first time since I'd known Theo, I just wanted him to disappear.

"You two know each other?" Tara asked politely.

I wanted to roll my turtleneck all the way up over my face and just hide. For one, I should have known better— of course I would see Theo there at his home ski mountain. I hadn't considered it because I thought he would be well on his way to Canada or wherever by now. Besides, I never thought he'd move on so quickly, but I supposed I shouldn't have been surprised. Tara was stunning, and she skied. Our time together hadn't been a serious relationship for him. It was all in my head. I took a deep breath and finally turned around.

"Oh, hey, Theo! What a small world." I immediately regretted stating the obvious— Sage Mountain was a town of 30,000 residents. Of *course,* it was a small world.

"Tara, this is Claire, uhh…"

Tara raised an eyebrow, putting two and two together that I was *that* Claire.

"Hey, that rhymes!"

Blake's friend released a little steam from the pressure cooker by cracking a dumb joke. It worked, and I chuckled at Theo's fumbling for words, if only for a moment.

Realizing how bad it looked, like I was casing out my ex-boyfriend's new girlfriend, I took the chance to speak. "I had no clue that you and Theo were… dating. I mean, we only broke up a month ago and, umm, not that you shouldn't be dating…" I felt so lame in my choice of words, so I just cut them off. At least Tara's expression showed she believed me.

"Wow, yeah, what a coincidence. Claire just took a beginner's ski lesson with me. I had no idea."

Tara stood there, stoic as she spoke. Though her words felt like a jab, with a heavy emphasis on *beginners,* I didn't feel that she intended them to be. I knew how many thoughts were going through my mind, so I could only imagine hers. Just then, I felt an arm go around me.

"Hi, I'm Blake."

The handsome man was now next to me, and I watched as he held out his hand to Theo, and they shook. The sweat broke out on my upper lip as I realized he was now squeezing his arm tight around my shoulder. I couldn't form a word, but I looked over at Blake and thanked him profusely with my eyes. I could only hope he was a mind reader.

"Well, it was lovely meeting you both. But I've promised Claire lunch after her lesson." He turned to me. "Shall we get out of this dump and go somewhere nice?"

Caught off guard by his joke, I laughed a little too hard, considering if that place wasn't a five-star hotel, it was a six, or maybe even a ten star. I nodded. "I can't go too far, as we have another ski lesson after lunch, but I think you'll like the chicken pasta here. It's good. I promise." I had heard this from an online review that I had read the night before, but it definitely gave me much-needed street credentials.

"Whatever you wish."

He turned us, and we walked towards the Peaks Lounge, the swankiest restaurant in the place. Once we turned the corner and they were out of sight and earshot, I nearly cried in thanking him. "You have no idea how much that helped me! Thank you so much, Blake! I owe you big time."

I gave him a hug, careful not to linger on his muscular frame for too long. From what I could tell, Blake had a great physique. He wasn't as tall as Theo's six-foot-two body. I guessed around five-eleven. For the first time, I realized I was staring into the dreamy green eyes of a man who was physically my "type," if there was such a thing. In my daydreams, I had always pictured having red-haired children. Here was a man who held some of the recessive gene, like myself. This made him quite literally the man of my (day) dreams. But if Theo taught me anything, a relationship should never be based on looks.

"Well, I am hungry, and you said I would like the chicken pasta, so let's start with that?"

I joyfully agreed, and as we entered the Peaks Lounge, I saw a big group from church. "Do you want to meet my people?" I asked Blake, to which he eagerly said "yes." I pointed them out and Mickey waved us over as they welcomed us to their table.

"Hey guys, this is Blake. We met a few days ago when I slipped and fell if you can believe it." Several of the kids burst out in laughter.

"Yeah, we can believe it, 'clumsy Claire.'"

It was a silly nickname that they overheard Mickey using once, but I thought it was just as funny, thankfully. It didn't bother me an ounce.

"We also met briefly before that, if you count the piano bar, Claire?"

I shot a glance at Tamara, who had instantly cocked her eyebrow in surprise, as if saying, "*The piano guy?*"

"Yes, of course I do. I wasn't sure if you remembered, is all."

"How could I forget?"

My pulse quickened as he looked at me. Blake was a person who could maintain eye contact, and I wasn't used to it in the least.

"I certainly can't." My voice lowered, and I looked away, not ready to explore outside of this conversation while I was standing in front of everyone I knew. Blake pulled out my chair, and I took a seat as he sat down next to me. The server came over to us the instant we sat down.

"Two chicken pastas, then?" I looked at Blake, and he nodded in reply.

Somehow, he and Mickey were already discussing spring baseball fantasy league picks. I excused myself to wash up. I couldn't believe what had just transpired. A perfect stranger just made me look a lot less pathetic in front of my ex and his gorgeous new girlfriend— a stranger that I'd now met two times before.

Chapter 6

When I returned to the table, the kids started shuffling out to check out the basement movie room and arcade. Mickey and Tamara decided they would go with them.

"We can't leave them unsupervised, Mick." Tamara nudged Mickey.

"But they are both in their thirties," Mickey razzed us, pretending that his wife was referring to Blake and I having lunch together and before they left, Tamara winked at me. I knew she would expect a full recap of this exchange the moment we were done, so I smiled back at her.

Our conversation took off like a rocket. Blake had questions about the youth group, and I filled him in on the bonding retreat that I was blessed to join. When the food arrived, it triggered other discussions for him and before long,

I was sharing my childhood fear of tomatoes and my preference for how eggs should be cooked. But I had questions too, and I it wasn't long before I started firing them off, so I started as politely as possible.

"Tell me about you."

"Shall I start from the beginning?" He ran his fingers through his wavy auburn hair. "I am here for a guy's ski trip. My buddy who made the wisecrack about your names rhyming, that's Timothy. This is technically his bachelor party. He is marrying his fiancé, Courtney, on Valentine's Day. Isn't that cute?" As he smiled, I saw a sincere twinkle in his eye. It *was* cute. "I live in Denver. I'm thirty-two years old, never married, and I would like three children. What a weird question to ask someone you just met." He cracked up laughing, knowing full well I *did not* ask him that.

"So, you must come here often, then. What is it, four hours away?"

"About that, yeah. I come up here occasionally. I was here a few weeks ago to scope out which place to stay for this trip; hence, our brief, but magical encounter playing Chopsticks."

He winked at me again, and I felt all the signals in my brain misfire. That guy was *smooth*– so much, in fact, that I nearly forgot about his relationship status.

"And… your girlfriend?"

He squinted his eyes together in confusion.

"The bartender."

He slowly nodded before bursting into laughter, recalling the exchange. "Ah, no, definitely not my girlfriend. That would be fifty shades of weird and probably illegal."

My eyebrows raised at his laughter, anticipating his explanation for what was so funny.

"That is my cousin, Sheila. We are only a month apart in age. Sheila's always been like a sister to me. She just moved here for the season, and before that, she lived with Sasha, Timothy's fiancé, in Denver. She's the hugging type, and now I can't wait to tell her someone thought we were *together*. I bet she will never do it again. I am about as single as it gets." He was cracking up left and right.

"Is that so?" Though I still wasn't sure where this exchange was leading to, I was glad to know he didn't have a girlfriend.

"Yes. I haven't had a relationship in a long time. Between life and work, I don't know… I guess I haven't really been looking."

We continued to talk and despite my best efforts to do a deep dive on just why that gorgeous man was single, before I knew it, the conversation shifted back to me, and I had told him everything: about getting dumped, turning thirty, and learning how to ski at my therapist's suggestion; about getting fired after my design for the new Sage Mountain Airport lounge got rejected by my boss, and how she had called it "cliché," and how hurtful that had been.

It seemed like he wanted to say something when I finished spewing out my life story, but he remained silent. The conversation fell flat, but the chemistry between us was palpable. It was right then when I saw I was ten minutes late for the second half of my ski lesson.

"Shoot. I better go. It was great chatting with you and thanks again for saving me back there. I'll see you on the slopes, if Tara will still have me, that is!"

"I hope to see you again, Claire."

My cheeks flushed, and I felt myself lingering. Truthfully, I would ditch Tara in a heartbeat to spend more time with that man, but I wasn't there for that. I was there for the commitment I made to skiing and for the grace of God that Mickey invited me there to ski for free. And because of that, I was there representing my church. I was about to kneel in prayer for the strength to walk away when my phone rang. Mickey was wondering where I was.

"Uh oh. I need to go. See you later, Blake." I tore out of the Peaks Lounge, racing until I made it back to the fireplace. The group was nowhere to be found. Then, I realized they wouldn't be waiting for me in the lobby. I ran down the stairs to the ski boot room where I found my entire group dressed and geared up. I shook my head in shame.

"It's not what it looks like, guys. I totally lost track of time while I was, umm…"

"Mhmmm." Mickey dramatically crossed his arms and shook his head. "Kids, this is what not marrying your high school sweetheart amounts to. The first good looking guy with fantastic taste in baseball that you romantically run into at a ski resort, you forget all about why you're here in the first place…"

The adults in the room were roaring in laughter.

"Okay, okay. Mickey is just *so* funny! Now, before we go out, since I've already made us late, let's say a prayer together. Who wants to lead?"

We all joined hands as our teen Kianna led us in a beautiful moment.

"Dear Lord, We thank you for bringing us all together for such a special week over our Christmas break. We ask for your protection on the slopes, especially since Mickey is not as good as he thinks he is, and at his age, we are really worried he will get injured. Also, we think Claire's new boyfriend is cool. We pray he is better than her last. In your name, Amen."

Mickey and I stood in silence for a moment, staring at each other with a blank expression when Kianna's mom, one of our other chaperones, stifling back her laughter, scolded her daughter. "Kianna, we don't pray things like that!"

A group of boys started making an impression of Mickey on skis. It made me laugh so hard that I had tears rolling down my face. It wasn't until Tara and two other instructors walked by that we knew we better get a move on. I was still giggling until I saw Tara's face when she turned to greet us at the bottom of the bunny hill.

"Okay, gang. Let's do a few more runs to perfect those 'Pizza' and 'French Fries' maneuvers. Claire, want to hold back for just a minute?"

I nodded and motioned for the teens to go to the magic carpet. "I'll meet you guys back down here and do the next run with you."

They were gone halfway through my sentence, eager to get back on the slopes. In light of an impending conversation with Tara, for once, there was nothing more I wanted to do than join them.

"I just wanted to 'clear the air,' so to speak." Her implied use of air quotes made me smile since she was wearing mitten style gloves, and I couldn't see her fingers. "I didn't know Theo was your ex-boyfriend. I wouldn't have let that interaction happen if I had. He told me how hard you took the breakup."

I raised my eyebrows at that, but I supposed I wasn't surprised. If Blake had asked about Theo, I would have told him anything he wanted to know as well. It was the same thing.

"Thanks, Tara. I think we were both blindsided by what just transpired. Don't worry about it; let's just move on."

"Oh, that makes me so happy to hear you say that, Claire! I would love to just start over fresh with you. When I met Theo a few months ago, we had no idea that our friendship would grow into a romance. My point of all that was… I hope you don't blame me for how things turned out, because I never intended to be a home wrecker."

Her eyes were watering now, as if she was on the verge of tears, but she was smiling, as if her atonement was telling me. I hadn't registered her words in my mind yet. My legs quivered as I slowly teetered back and forth on my skis. A fall was imminent, I could tell.

"A few months ago? How long have you been together?" Surely, I misheard Tara.

"Just a few weeks. Well, on my birthday, to be specific. December 13th."

She smiled apologetically, as I took the information in. "Not to rub it in that it was so soon after your breakup, but when he said you'd parted ways, well, truthfully, I was expecting him to ask me out sooner."

We broke up just three days before they got together. Was that not long enough? Or had Theo told her and me two different things? I was starting to wonder. A familiar feeling took hold of my gut as Tara glided away on her skis. The wind had been knocked out of me. The last time this happened, I was roller skating in a friend's garage when I was ten. I fell so hard on my rear-end, that I couldn't breathe right for a few minutes. While I was still upright, I couldn't see straight, my legs were weak, and if I hadn't just found out my ex was courting another woman while we were still together, I would have surmised this to a stroke.

It was all I could do to excuse myself politely, telling Kianna's mom I wasn't feeling well suddenly, and needed to make it back into the lodge.

The first person I saw when I went inside was Tamara. She looked up at me expectantly.

"Claire! Are you okay? You don't look well." She got up and motioned to a chair for me to sit in. "What's wrong?"

"Theo… was talking to another woman while we were still together. With my ski instructor. Tara."

Tamara's jaw dropped in disbelief. I may have been quickly moving past Theo, but the feelings of this fresh wound were just too much to bear. Before I knew it, I had told Tamara the entire story, including my reason for learning to ski, Theo's supposed reason for dumping me, and then about getting fired from my job. The more I told it, the more exhausting it felt.

"Oh, Claire. You've really been through it, haven't you? I'm so sorry."

She sat with me in silence as I let a few tears fall. But with each tear, the negativity was released from my heart.

"If there's anything I've learned in life, it's that 'this too shall pass.' There's nothing in life that God can't heal. He has a greater plan for you. And I believe it's starting sooner than you think."

I looked over at Tamara and hugged her. "Thank you for being such a good friend to me."

She was looking at something behind me as she smiled.

"How's my perfect and beautiful-in-every-way wife?" Mickey's voice rang behind me.

"My blood sugar is good. No need to walk on eggshells, Mickey. Unless, of course, you want to."

We both giggled. Mickey and his wife had the greatest sense of humor. Their compatibility made them such a joyful couple to be around.

"Listen, Mick. The kids were right. You need to work on your core skills some more. Why don't you and Claire trade places? Spending a little more time on the basics might do you some good."

Mickey didn't question a thing. "Sure, darling. And then I'll give you a foot rub tonight if you promise not to make me sleep on the floor. Capeesh?"

They were both cackling as he gave her a kiss and nodded to me to switch.

"Thanks, guys. Mickey, which instructor are you with again?"

"Trevor. Black hair, white boots. You can't miss him."

And Mickey was right; I couldn't miss him. In fact, I was a little worried that I hadn't seen him until just then, given that his pants were neon tie-dyed.

"Trevor? My name is Claire. If you don't mind, I've just switched places with Mickey and would like to join this lesson for the duration. I'm still a beginner, though, so it's okay if you have nothing for me."

Trevor pointed to the chairlift. "All the kids are going up. There's two ways down: take a right for the green run. I'll be right behind you." For having such a fun way of dressing, he sure wasn't exuding joy to talk to.

Filled with nerves, I lined up to get on the two-seater chair. I had to choose between facing Tara and confronting the pain of betrayal or taking on a more challenging slope than the bunny hill. I went with the second choice. To my horror, I realized they weren't loading any single riders up. None of the teens were around, meaning I would have to ride up with a stranger. I counted all the riders ahead of me, and it worked out that I would ride up with the woman ahead of me. She had baby pink pants and a purple coat. She was about my mother's age and looked cheerful. About a second later, a friend joined her in line.

"There you are. One more run?" The woman nodded.

I peeked over my shoulder. The man behind me was Timothy, Blake's friend. He was totally immersed in his phone and didn't look up from it. Okay, that wasn't so bad, I guessed.

When it was our turn to get on the chair, things were moving slowly and the lift tech informed us it was because a group of kids were riding the lift. "They need extra time to offload."

"And how would I go about getting extra time?" I laughed, nervously.

"Just do this motion." He showed me a bobbing thumbs down.

"Thanks." We gently took off upward, and Timothy put the bar down on our laps. "Timothy, right? I'm Claire. Blake told me about you and your upcoming wedding. Congratulations."

He grinned ear to ear. "Ahh, yes. Thank you. I can't wait. It was cool for Blake to bring us out here for the week. Or, his dad, anyway."

My ears perked up. "What do you mean?"

"Well, I mean, his dad owns the place, so he just had to make a phone call to the front desk, and we had three rooms and a week's worth of ski passes. Pretty sweet deal, if you ask me. His dad is the greatest. He was like a dad to me growing up. Can't ski to save his life, but loves the idea of it, so he buys up all these resorts."

I was at a loss for words. Blake didn't think to tell me any of this earlier? "Is his dad… James Walker?" The CEO at my job. At my *old* job, that was.

"Yes, that's him. Do you know him?" Timothy looked me dead in the eyes.

"I do. Well, I know of him. I just got fired from the design firm for Sage Mountain Resort and Airport because he wouldn't have liked my ideas, actually."

"Ouch. I'm sorry about that."

My mind was racing. Did that mean Blake worked with his dad, too? Did he already know about me, my designs, my firing? This was feeling painfully weird.

"There's Melanie."

I followed Timothy's gloved finger's direction to a woman with eyes of emerald that were so dazzling that I could see them from the chairlift. She was at a standstill as she looked at her watch. Her goggles sat around her cute, fuzzy hat and her long, thick, brown hair was perfectly spilling over her white coat. She was gorgeous in every sense of the word, and the feelings of dread came creeping back. Part of me didn't want to know this woman, as I was feeling emotionally damaged, and she was like looking into the sun. I'd half expected her to be Theo's new girlfriend if he wasn't already linked with the stunning Tara, but alas, I was a curious creature. I turned back to Timothy and croaked out a minor question. "Who's Melanie?"

He squinted his brow together. "Blakes ex… Didn't he tell you? She's here skiing with her family."

My heart sank to the bottom of my gut. It felt like it was pressing on my bladder, or the hot chocolate consumption had finally caught up to me. Either way, I didn't feel good about any of this. "No, I guess not."

Timothy nodded at my reply. Not that he needed to tell me– Blake didn't owe me any explanation whatsoever. We'd only just met. Still, the triple whammy of information I'd just uncovered was sickening.

Before I could contemplate asking any more questions, we made it to the top, and I'd forgotten all about the signal for the lift techs to slow the chair down. Thankfully, Timothy hadn't forgotten, and we came to a glacial pace.

"Take it easy, Claire."

The second he disembarked from the chair, he tore off to the left. I went straight, going slightly uphill, as I couldn't stop. My skis were going out of control, but I didn't want to bring any attention to the fact out of embarrassment. I was able to turn around once I slowed enough and came to a complete stop so I could assess where I was. Trevor had said to go right. Did he mean when I faced the chair lift or when it was to my back? The panic washed over me. Where was the sign marking the runs? I awkwardly skied over to the left. Not a sign in sight. Then, to the right. I saw a sign off in the distance, so I went a little further until I realized I was at the top of the run. I couldn't turn back; there were too many people, and the ski patroller said no loitering. I knew it always looked the worst from that angle, so I went for it: my first solo run on that trip, feeling insecure and painfully inexperienced, and without an instructor to help.

I started out by making the pizza formation and attempting small turns, just like Tara had shown me. I couldn't quite muster the part about lifting a foot up without almost falling, so I left that behind. When it got steep, I did smaller, more frequent turns. My biggest concern was getting run over by another skier. If I could go down without looking over my shoulder, it would've been so much better. Distraction came when someone called out my name.

"Claire!" It was the man of the hour: Blake. "How's your ski lesson going?" He looked all around us. "Are you out here alone?" Suddenly, he spun around on his skis and was sliding down a small slope *backwards*. "I call this my swoon turn. Does it work?"

I laughed. "That would depend. Are you trying to swoon me? Because right now there's a lot I don't know about you."

His smile turned into a frown. "What happened?" he asked, coming to a stop while I dug my poles into the snow, leaning on them to take a much-needed break.

"Oh, nothing. Timothy just told me about your dad owning the company I just got fired from. Owning this resort— heck, this whole town. Oh, and your stunning ex-girlfriend who just so happens to be here for the week. Meanwhile, I'm up here stuck on the glorified bunny hill, in a panic about getting to the bottom, and sweating all my makeup off in the process. I just can't compete with all these women who can ski so well and still look absolutely perfect." I huffed, taking a breath from my mini meltdown. "That's all."

His frown turned deeper. "I'm sorry, Claire. I was going to tell you all those things, but I couldn't figure out how. After you said you were fired, I didn't want to sour our relationship."

"What relationship? We just met, Blake. We don't have one. I told you who my father was. That would have been a great opportunity for you to chime in."

"Okay, okay. I know. And I'm sorry, Claire. Can you forgive me for not telling you immediately who my dad is?"

I thought about it for a minute, pushing my skis as hard as I could into the pizza formation.

"You really need to watch your knees," Blake chimed in.

I was drenched in sweat, and he looked fresh as a daisy.

He gracefully skied closer to me and saw me up close, stifling back a laugh. "I love how serious you're taking these skiing lessons. I find it very endearing. You really put your heart and soul into what you set out to accomplish, I can tell." He gave a sincere smile, but when I didn't give him one in return, he frowned.

"I guess."

"Do you trust me?"

"I— I don't know." I felt my blood sugar dropping fast. Where was everyone? Mickey? Chaperones? The snow cat to take me down in the sled of shame? "I'm just feeling completely exhausted." This was so tiring, and the run looked like it kept getting longer and longer.

"I know how you feel. I get it. Here, let me help you. I promise to take care of you, Claire."

I weighed my options: Staying in place or getting out of this situation now. I took the latter. "Okay, fine."

Blake linked our arms together, and he placed his skis on the outside of mine. While he wasn't holding me close to his body, I felt secure. Within seconds, we were gliding down the mountain at a perfect speed. "Just stay still and keep your skis together. I got you," he said in my ear as my legs instinctively tried to do some work. I closed my eyes for a moment, taking the words in. Doing what he said would require my letting go of the control I desperately wanted to keep. But I was getting nowhere trying to control that situation and was only making it harder on myself. The same went for many aspects of my life. I felt myself melt into his arms, putting the weight of my body into his as I let that man— one whom I did not know, but admittedly, wanted to— help me.

When we reached the end of the run, he began to gradually release my arms. "You know what to do. Don't panic, Claire. Just ski."

He released me from his grip, and I kept up the momentum, gliding at an easy pace as the ground turned flat beneath me. When I came to a natural stop, I looked back at him, and he smiled and clapped. With Blake helping me, the trip had become effortless and without physical and emotional strain. I thanked God for sending Blake to me at that very moment to help in my time of need.

I took off my gloves and unhooked my skis while Blake took two strides and met me where I was, my legs shaking in the aftermath of the trauma of feeling afraid and stranded on the ski hill.

"Claire, I'd like to tell you a few more things about me." He paused, waiting for me to accept the conversation.

"Okay, sure. I'm interested in what you have to say." Saying it out loud also admitted it to myself: The man had intrigued me. He had just witnessed me having a total meltdown and was then still interested in speaking to me.

"You see, my parents and I are kind of at a fork in the road. They want me to be living life on their timeline and I…"

He paused, releasing a big breath into the cold air. "Well, I just don't see things the same. I guess I'm just out here forging my path, and don't want everyone to decide who I am based on my father's company. Especially not this. I feel terrible that you were let go. But please, Claire. Let me make it up to you," he pled with his eyes, as well as his words. "You and I are both here this week, but so is your ex-boyfriend, who seems like a real piece of work. I saw him in the men's restroom styling his hair. I know just his type."

I didn't know what he was getting at, but the jab at Theo made me feel defensive. "Lest we forget about *your* ex-girlfriend being here. Melanie? Yeah, it's the real icing on the cake, I'd say, unless you planned it that way. Unless you *want* to get back with her and speaking to me is now interrupting those plans?"

Blake shook his head. "It's not what you think, Claire. Yes, she is here until tomorrow, which is an unfortunate coincidence. Her parents were the only ones slighted in our very *mutual* breakup over a year ago. They will not quit meddling and always seem to plan these trips when we might run into each other. But believe me when I say there's no future where Melanie and I end up together. Trust me… We are two extremely different people. For instance, I want a family. She wants to move to India. I want to learn about competitive clay shooting. She doesn't believe in weapons. Our personalities clash, too. Melanie is a very serious person, and you can't take me anywhere because I'm always laughing." He put his hand on my shoulder. "But even if I liked all the things I don't, and I wanted to get back with her, she's already moved on and is dating a guy from the NFL."

I was surprised at his words and why he was speaking them, but it gave me relief knowing that she was not looking for love with Blake. Regardless, I was feeling a little embarrassed at my blowup. "Blake, you don't have to explain yourself. We've only just met, and I don't expect you— "

He cut me off. "I know I don't have to, but I want to tell you, Claire. You deserve to have people be upfront with you. That being said," he leaned closer and took my hands in his, "I have a proposal to make."

"A proposal?" He had my attention.

"If you think you can pretend to like me, I will be your pretend boyfriend for the rest of the week, so you can save face with your ex. What do you think about that? I mean, if you think you can stomach the thought of riding the chairlift with me, holding my hand… being my date on New Year's Eve…"

I thought about it for a minute as my legs quivered beneath me from overuse. I hadn't gotten as much exercise as I had hoped, but this was pushing my limits. All I wanted to do was get inside and sit in front of the warm fireplace with a cup of hot chocolate.

"I don't know, Blake. I mean, it sounds like it could be fun, and I appreciate it, but how would it be believable?

"Easy: We can't do this halfway. We need to make a full-fledged commitment. I want it to look so real that even *we* forget it's not. If I promise to give it my all for your sake, will you give it your all for mine?"

I wondered what he would get out of this, but even so, the agreement *was* just what I needed to feel better around Theo. "Okay."

Blake cheered as he jumped up and down, somehow even doing that perfectly on his skis. "Thank you, Claire, for letting me make this right. If we do it correctly, I think we are going to really have some fun. Just you wait." He grinned and held his hand out. "Oh, there's one more thing." I cocked my eyebrow, wondering what else there could be on earth that we hadn't covered. "When you said that you can't compete with women who ski, meaning Melanie and Tara… I just want to say, I never asked you to compete with them. And I never would."

Watching him gracefully slide away, taking any remaining words I had with him, I wondered just who that man was. He differed from anyone else I'd ever met, in the best way.

I was so eager to get back inside, I nearly cried when I took my ski boots off. What. A. Day. A group of the youth group moms and girls were urging me to accompany them to the hot tubs before dinner, and I couldn't think of anything better. "Let's do it, ladies."

*****

That night, I reflected on the proposal I had agreed to with Blake. Taking out my phone, I opened my social media to see a friend request waiting from him. I accepted because it would be weird not to be connected online to the man I was supposedly dating. Clicking on his profile, I scrolled through to see his pictures.

Blake had done it all: He was a world traveler; sailed the seven seas; experienced Michelin restaurants; talented at different sports; and was especially good at playing the piano, which I knew from experience. His charm was evident, even through the phone screen. I admitted to myself just how attracted I felt to Blake but in a much different way than to Theo.

Theo was built like a Grecian statue, and he knew it. There was nothing he loved more than showing off his physique. He looked in every mirror he had the chance to and never let a photo opportunity pass him by. Blake, on the other hand… Most of his photos were candid, and friends posted most of them. In fact, the only photo Blake had posted of himself was his profile picture of him at his college graduation and scenery photos of his travels. I could respect that.

Upon scrolling, I found a photo posted by Melanie. It was a picture of them standing at a golfing tournament together, presumably with her parents. I clicked on her profile to see she wasn't just dating a man from the NFL, but they were newly engaged. While I assumed he was a football player, I learned he was a football executive and a solid ten to fifteen years older than Melanie.

Going back to Blake's page, I felt closure with Melanie. While she was one of the most beautiful women I'd ever seen, neither Blake nor Melanie appeared to be interested in each other. I could let that go, writing it off as an awkward coincidence that she was there. "Not that any of it matters, because we aren't really dating after all…" I mumbled to myself before a final scroll of Blake's pictures, when my jaw truly dropped.

Apparently, Blake was a world-class skier…I couldn't believe my eyes when I saw the photo of him holding a trophy. He didn't post it, but a skiing association tagged him in the photo. It looked like he won the men's cup in a national slalom race two years prior. I felt impressed and worried at the same time. Tossing my phone to the side, I was impressed that he was so talented at, well, everything, yet worried because I wasn't. I just needed to get through that week and put my best ski boot forward.

"It just has to be believable that we are dating," I mumbled, trying to convince myself. "Then I can go back to my life and figure out what's next." The feeling of dread started to creep up as I considered just what could be next for me.

December 29th

The next morning, I woke up to my alarm. Getting up an hour prior to the teenagers was always my plan so that I could eat breakfast in the early morning, but once that it was in action, I felt groggy and like my face was puffy. Pulling on my bathrobe, I went over to the modest balcony in my room and opened the double doors for some fresh air and stumbled upon the most amazing sunrise.

As the sun slowly rose behind Sage Mountain, a peak known for its angular ridges and blunt shape of a narrow triangle, the fresh layer of powder that lay on every surface started sparkling. Little flakes blew off the roof, swirling around me. The colors in the sky were unbelievable as it lit, going from pinks to golds. I watched in awe, unaware of my cold feet and surroundings. I felt a tear fall down my cheek, both from the cold weather and the humbling beauty that God had shown me.

Alpenglow. I remembered my dad telling me about this term of colors in the sky when I was a kid. Though I could always be reliable with being on time, I was never much of an early riser. I was more of a sunset-chaser. But it was worth getting up for, as I vowed to enjoy it more frequently. Just then, I saw a skier in the distance make the way down a run. With no lifts running yet, that person must have hiked up. Each turn was perfectly carved through the powdery, sparkling white. While I watched, I felt that person's commitment to skiing was inspiring and found myself wanting to experience a sunrise ski. As our glowing orb of light arrived at its full form, and the skier was now out of sight, I slipped back inside, feeling refreshed at the experience.

After making a cup of coffee in the little machine in my room, I started sorting through my clothes to find what I was going to wear for the day. I chose a black turtleneck with thermal leggings to go under my ski pants and jacket. Black looked good on me when I wore a little mascara, otherwise it washed me out. So, that's what I decided to do.

No amount of mascara could conceal just how puffy I had looked that morning. Things spiraled out of control and by the time I was done with my makeup, I was wearing mascara, blush, bronzer, under-eye brightener, and a swipe of pink lip gloss. I wondered if it was too much but remembered that Tara wore a full face of makeup, and it didn't seem out of place at all. It's just that this was abnormal for me because I normally only wore it on special occasions. But then again, I had a new— er, *fake* boyfriend to show off to, and an ex to face, so the occasion was pretty unique.

Once I had my hat and gloves on, I headed down the hall, only to hear a door opening behind me.

"Good morning, Claire." Mayah, with her long, jet-black hair, was one of the older girls in the youth group at seventeen. "Do you want some coffee? I just made a pot."

My eyes widened to see she was drinking it black. "No, thank you, Mayah. I am more of a coffee-with-my-creamer type, I'm afraid." I laughed, not expecting to see such a young woman with a taste for black coffee.

"I used to think that, too, until we started getting our coffee direct from a grower in South America. It's completely fair-trade, organic, and it has hints of hazelnut. Once you drink this in its purest form, there's no going back to that sugary sludge that's served in coffee shops."

"Hmm. I don't think I'm ready for that kind of enlightening yet because I happen to relish my sludge. Well, I'm going to get some food."

Mayah nodded in agreement. "Great idea. Most of us are up if it's okay that we join you? We can be there in just a few minutes."

Though I'd planned on eating alone, it was a joy to be around the teens and I agreed, leaving Mayah to finish her fancy brew and head downstairs to reserve some seats. The breakfast buffet was already crowded, but fortunately, there were plenty of seats scattered in the back. I made a beeline for the area and took off my jacket and gloves while I waited. Only then did I look around.

To the left of me, I saw Timothy with two other men. Blake was not with them. Perhaps he slept in? I didn't get to think about it too long before noticing Theo and Tara eating together in a booth to the right of me. Unfortunately, Theo was facing me. I kept catching his gaze unintentionally, and it made me feel sad— not for dating him, not for even wanting to marry him, but for the lies I was uncovering, and for the deceiving he did to both Tara and me. I wrestled in my mind if and how I could tell her without it destroying her day. I saw Tara take Theo by the hand and then they moved seats so my back would be to them.

"Good morning," Blake's voice rang loudly as his bright eyes scanned my face, taking the seat across from me. I felt Theo's eyes on us instantly. "Would you like a coffee? I'm about to go get one." He had a dusting of snow on his jacket, and to my surprise, he reached his hand out to hold mine, just as Tara had done to Theo. *This dating may not be real, but it sure is fun*, I thought.

"Absolutely. I'll take a vanilla latte. Pretty please."

He nodded and gave my hand a squeeze, standing up. His dark reddish hair was so striking on his olive skin; he really was quite good looking.

"You got it, Claire. By the way, you look beautiful."

I felt my face redden at the compliment. Was this part of the act, or did he mean that? With no one around to enjoy the compliment other than myself, I decided he meant it.

"Thank you." I smiled from ear to ear. I had never met a man who was so unapologetic or bold in his compliments. At risk of ruining the moment by comparing Blake to Theo, I cleared my mind from my ex and savored Blake's words as the teenagers started shuffling in with Mickey and Tamara in tow. After everyone got their food, Blake returned with my coffee in hand.

"Good morning, guys." Blake acknowledged the group as he handed me the cup while Mickey immediately went for a fist bump.

"What's up, my man?" I was surprised at how friendly Mickey was with Blake already, considering Mickey barely spoke to Theo during our fourteen-month relationship. They exchanged platitudes, and I listened casually until Mickey's question caught me off guard. "Was that you out there tearing it up this morning?"

My eyes widened. Was the early morning skier, Blake?

"Oh, yeah. I didn't know I had an audience, man." Blake laughed as Tamara piped up.

"Make that an audience of two." Tamara waived her hand. "You must have gotten an early start this morning. How long did it take to hike up there?"

"About two hours. I started at four— just something I like to do now and then to get a little quiet time and clear my head. There's no greater church in the world than God's creation."

If just watching him this morning was an experience, I wondered what it would have been like to ski that. Wait… What was happening? Was this a genuine desire to ski bubbling up inside of me?

"Well, I better go join my group. Claire, I will see you on the slopes?" His sudden attention on me with his attractive face made my mind go blank. One of the teenage girls kicked my leg under the table.

"Yes, of course. Enjoy your breakfast." What a lame thing that was to say; did I work there or something? Blake nodded and went to join his group. When he was out of earshot, the girls started raving.

"He's so cute, Claire!"

"What a hunk."

"He's a real stone fox." Mickey's comment made us all laugh hysterically. Though he said it sarcastically, I caught Tamara's eyes a moment later, and she gave me a wink and thumbs up of approval. I felt a wave of guilt and sadness that it was all a ruse.

"Alright, everyone. Let's finish things up. You all need to be in the gear room in ten minutes for the instructors. Parents? Who would like to lead a morning prayer?"

Changing the subject and chasing a sugar high from the pancakes, Vicki led us in prayer, and then I got up to get one more coffee before the day started. Part of me felt weird about this fake-dating scheme, but Blake had the free will to do as he pleased. And it was helping my loneliness in the wake of Theo also being there with his new girlfriend, so truthfully, I didn't want it to end.

Later that morning, Trevor, my ski instructor in the tie-dye pants, was helping us with our stops when I saw Blake ski down in front of me. My attention was honed in on him when he disappeared inside the lodge, turning my attention back to the lesson.

"Claire, it's your turn to try it out. Ski down a little way, pick up some speed, and try it."

I went for it without hesitation. As I picked up a little speed, I abruptly pointed my skis sideways, using the edges to stop.

"Great job, Claire. Now let's head to the lift so we can put it all together."

The instructor was the first one to get to the lift, leaving the rest of us behind. He was standing in line directly behind Tara, and they ended up sharing the same chair. I looked around, expecting to see Theo somewhere, but he was nowhere to be found. Instead, I saw Blake coming over.

"Hey, Claire. Are you up for taking a run with me?"

"Sure, if a ski pro like you doesn't mind that I'm working on my turns and stops," I teased.

He leaned into his poles, looking over at me. "I think it's amazing you're learning to ski, Claire," he smiled. "And there was something I wanted to ask you." We loaded onto the two-seater chair lift, and as we gained elevation, I turned and asked him what that was. "My parents are arriving in town today, and I was wondering if you would like to join us for dinner tomorrow night? If you're even able to, with your plans and all. It would be at seven, if you can."

He seemed a little nervous in his question. Meeting the parents? The line of our agreement became blurred in an instant. Or was this what he would gain from our arrangement? "Sure, I'd love to. Mickey had mentioned us having dinner together at five tomorrow, so I can moonlight on both occasions."

What a relief that his was so much later in the evening. I needed to remember that I was there first for the group. Despite not being a chaperone, I still liked to be available to them, not for my own interests. But since Mickey and Tamara approved, and there were plenty of other parents, I knew it would be okay to be absent after dinner.

"Wonderful. I'll have a car pick you up at 6:45. It will be at their home over in the Blueberry Basin."

"Ooh, fancy. They have a ski-in/out home here? I didn't know that."

Blake almost looked embarrassed. "Yeah, you know my dad doesn't ski, but he insists on a collection of ski properties. It's almost hoarding at this point."

"Must be convenient since you ski. You can go to them, I mean."

Blake shook his head. "No, not really… I live on my own dime. I love my parents, but I am completely independent of them. While I am welcome to stay at one of their properties, I want to make my own opportunities and experiences."

"Oh, I thought… I mean, Timothy said something about you guys staying here because of your dad…?"

"Yes, he owns the hotel. He called to secure the rooms, but we paid for them. We got an employee discount, at least!" Blake laughed.

It was impressive to learn that despite having unlimited resources in his family, he was determined to forge his own path. Reflecting upon my own feelings, I was so hung up on what I thought my father wanted for my life that I could barely consider what I wanted. I had a feeling Blake would never let that get in his way. There was so much I could learn from Blake.

"So, what is it that you do?" While I felt he knew everything about me, I still knew little about him.

"It sounds pretty cliché, but I work for my dad's company. It pains me to learn that we were almost coworkers and didn't know it." He shot me a smile. "But I work on the finance side of things. I'm on the company's team of financial advisors. I enjoy it, but I've been gaining much more interest in the real estate side of things as of late. I started investing in properties a few years ago, and it's been really fulfilling."

"Like what kind? Don't tell me you're the guy buying up all the condos for short-term rentals…?" I timidly asked, giving him a playful punch in the arm.

"No, nothing like that. Nothing residential. I've been getting commercial spaces and leasing to nonprofits. Right now, I have an animal shelter, a church, and a senior center. My favorite way to spend a day is actually hitting up all three and spending time with them. David is the pastor at Elk Valley Church, and I really connect with his messages. He can explain things in terms I understand, which is a lifesaver. Then I spend hours with the kitties at Fremont Animal Shelter. I'm this close to taking home a dozen, let me tell you." He held up an inch sign with his hand.

"Ahh, you're a cat guy? I'd have taken you for a golden retriever lover." At least that's what I was projecting, considering that was my dream family dog.

"Oh, I'd take a handful of goldens, too, don't worry. I have plenty of room in my heart for all pets. I'm looking forward to getting a dog next year since my lease is up at my condo, and I'm looking to buy."

"That's great." Every bone in my body wanted to offer help when he picked out that future dog, but I held back. "And what about the senior center? What's that all about?"

"Now that's entertainment. I like to go there on Tuesdays because that's when it's line dancing night. You think it gets rowdy at bars? You ain't seen nothing until you watch Marsha get her two-step on." We both laughed at the visual. "I'll have to take you sometime." It wasn't lost on me that he was making future plans, but then again, nothing was set in stone.

Looking at Blake in wonderment, I felt an out-of-body experience coming on. "Okay, so Mr. Perfect-looking is also perfect on the inside?" I slammed my hand over my mouth. I didn't mean to say that out loud!

Blake started cracking up laughing. "Well, I don't know about any of that. I am an extremely flawed sinner, just like everyone else. But I'm elated to know you think I look perfect… because the feeling is mutual, Claire. You're a pretty fun girl to fake date."

I was relieved to be wearing a full face of makeup and that my cheeks were already rosy from the cold, considering my face liked to betray me with redness any chance it got. At least then he wouldn't see the difference, and I could keep my poker face about me. Except for one problem: I was grinning ear to ear.

When we made it to the top, Blake insisted I go down first. "But I'm not fast and you'll be waiting around." I pled with him that I would meet him at the bottom, but he insisted.

"There's nowhere else I'd rather be, Claire. Go ahead, take your time."

For the first time in my skiing experience, I felt safe. Safe to go at my own speed. Safe to try, knowing that if I needed help, it would be there. And that's what I did. I left the world behind me and put all my focus into carving my way down. I remembered watching Blake that morning; he made it look so effortless.

Tara had given me a tip on turning: to lift the inner ski ever so slightly. I felt brave enough to put that into play. It was difficult to muster the day before, but I was ready to give it another shot. As I attempted it with a little more speed, I found it easier than I thought, but I was also on a flat spot.

Earlier, Trevor had said to keep making turn after turn. He called it "making a curve." He said, "Every time you turn, make another curve."

Saying it on repeat really stuck out in my mind, and I started repeating it. "Make a curve. Make a curve." And I did. My skiing went from exasperating to exhilarating. While I was only going marginally faster, I felt at ease. My back went from a hunched, stressed position to fluid and upright. The crisp sounds of my skis' sharp edges were a familiar song as I cut through the powder. Every part of that gave me confidence and healing for my heart. When I finally made it to the bottom, Blake was trailing right behind me.

"You did amazing, Claire. You have a beautiful form."

"Thank you. I think watching you ski this morning helped that."

He looked at me with curiosity. "You saw me? Did everyone see me? I thought I was silent as a mouse." He yawned as he spoke. It was clear the early day and uphill hike through the deep snow were catching up with him.

"I didn't know it was you until Mickey asked you at breakfast. I was watching the sunrise. You were just an added piece of art to that."

He looked at me with a sparkle in his eyes but was silent for a moment. "Goodness, I'm tired. I think I'll be paying for that the rest of the day unless I go take a nap." He took his gloves off and rubbed his eyes. "Thank you for watching me, Claire. Though I didn't know it at the time, I like the fact that you saw me. It's like a shared experience for us now."

"Yeah, I guess it is. Enjoy your nap. I'm going to catch up with my instructor, so I'll see you later." Mild panic washed over me as I realized I had nothing to wear to his parents in Blueberry Basin, but then I remembered the swanky boutique in the lodge had women's clothing. I hoped they had something I could afford.

Blake turned towards the lodge and paused, looking over his shoulder. His eye contact held an intensity that I quickly got lost in. "You know, Claire… I've done all the skiing in the world— Japan, Italy, Swiss Alps. And yet, following you at a snail's pace in Wyoming is my favorite."

*****

At lunch, more of the parents came up from town to join us since it was Saturday, and some were off work. Tamara and I could catch up, alone, at our own table while we had hot soup together. I told her everything, starting with Blake's proposal of fake dating; his father being the CEO; and the invitation to their home for dinner. When I was done, Tamara didn't miss a beat.

"You're going to need something to wear to your fake boyfriend's parents tomorrow. I bet that will be one classy affair." She abruptly stood up, taking inventory over the kids. I followed her lead, realizing she meant we needed to find something to wear *right then.* There were more adults than we knew what to deal with, so we agreed to check out the boutique on the other side of the lodge.

The store had beautiful glass double doors that were heavy to open, but once we did, we were met with an incredible fragrance of cinnamon, vetiver, and warmth. They had a gorgeous fireplace on the west wall with sparkling glass stones inside. Tamara quickly went to the smaller-than-I'd-hoped selection of women's clothing and began sliding through. "Claire- this would really play up your eyes! I think they are your best feature. You will look beautiful in something like this." She held up a boat neck black sweater dress that looked like it came just above the knee, so it would give warmth and a flirty style. "And what size shoe are you? I brought some black heeled boots that my feet are way too swollen to wear."

I loved the dress. Immediately checking the price tag, I found the price high, but easy to swallow. And, since we knew we were the same shoe size, there was one less thing I had to worry about. As soon as I tried it on, I loved it. "What do you think? Will it work?"

Tamara laughed and vigorously nodded her head. "Girl, are you kidding me? You slay in that dress! It's not too tight, not too short, or overly revealing. It makes your eyes pop, especially with your makeup today. You just need some hosiery. Don't worry, you could wear that to church next week, so it's not just a onetime wear."

At Tamara's encouragement, I bought the dress and excitedly went with her to retrieve the boots. They were perfect slouch, mid-calf boots made of a soft velvet material. "Do you have a long necklace?" Tamara pulled out a small selection of jewelry. "I figured at least one night here, I will go out for a solo dessert date with Mickey, so I came prepared." She held up a long chain that had little assorted flowers, shapes and pearls. It was black and white. She layered it once around my neck and let the rest hang low. "That's a wrap. You look perfect."

Thanking her wholeheartedly, she said my excitement was contagious and that the moment I got back, I was to text her about everything that happened. "I have to get through the rest of this day first, and all of tomorrow, with no idea how I'll manage that. Only ten minutes have passed since I last checked. For a fake relationship, this is the giddiest I've ever been." We giggled our way to my room, where I dropped off the new dress, necklace, and boots, before making our way back downstairs to rejoin the group.

Instead of getting back on skis, I sat with Tamara until the rest of the group finished, as she had been sitting it out alone so far. We got hilarious videos of Mickey skiing with the kids, we talked about her pregnancy, and we enjoyed each other's company. When it was the group's dinner time, we had reserved the largest table in the dining room so we could all sit together with the other parents. The Saturday night dinner special was Ravioli di Aragosta, and I savored the garlic bread. At six, Tamara announced she was going to lie down for a while. I also felt exhaustion hit and excused myself.

Though everyone was so preoccupied, only a few noticed, including Mickey.

I walked Tamara to her room and said goodnight and made my way to my own. The carbs were hitting my brain faster than I could walk, and when I turned the corner of the hallway, I almost ran smack dab into Melanie.

"Excuse me, I'm so sorry." Nerves ran down my fingers as I was looking at my fake boyfriend's very real ex-girlfriend, face to face.

"No worries, dear." Her brows squinted together as her smile widened. "Hey. I'm Melanie." She extended her hand with impeccably manicured nails, and I shook it.

"Claire."

"I saw you with Blake. I hope I'm not overstepping here, but I…" she trailed off.

"You dated; I know. It's nice to meet you." And it was nice to meet her. It certainly piqued my curiosity. She exhaled, her eyes widening.

"I dated Blake for about five months, nearly a year and a half ago. And it appears you've found your way into his heart now, and I just want to say I'm thrilled for you… And I'm sorry to be here. My parents can't accept my new relationship because he's older. But I want you to know I'm not here for Blake. Frankly, I'm embarrassed that my parents invited me to this, knowing he would be here."

I had questions and wanted answers. "How did you know he would be here? I don't understand."

"Sasha, the bride? Her mom and my mom are best friends… So, here we are."

It all came together at that moment. I felt Melanie's struggles. Though they differed from my own, I considered what she must have been feeling. "I'm sorry your parents are struggling with your relationship." I thought of my own parents and considered how they were going to accept the fateful news that Theo and I were no longer. "Maybe they will come around."

"Thankfully, we all saw you and Blake together, so now that he's not a single guy, I think they just might. We have a lot to work through, starting with their fears about my marrying an older man. I'm just really looking forward to going home tomorrow. I've got the red-eye flight booked, and it can't come soon enough. And I wish you the best with Blake. He's a wonderful man. Judging by his character, I know you must be an incredible woman. He and I weren't right for each other, but I've prayed he would find you. And it looks like he did."

I considered coming clean with her about our *arrangement*, but she hurriedly tiptoed away, vanishing around a corner. After taking inventory of my mind, I crept back into my room. Melanie was a kind soul, and while I believed Blake that she wasn't here for him, it was lovely speaking to her face to face. Checking the time; it was still early, 7:30 p.m. I lay down for a moment, fully intending to get back up and go play board games with the teens and their parents, but I ended up falling asleep. When I woke up, I was still in all my daytime clothes, and it was 3:45 in the morning.

Chapter 8

December 30th

I rubbed my eyes, remembering only then I had applied copious amounts of makeup. "Darn it," I said under my breath. I went to the bathroom and washed up before walking over to the balcony and getting fresh air. As I slipped out, I took a moment to enjoy the stars in all of their glory. I said a prayer of gratitude for all God had shown me, that week especially.

"Thank You, Lord, for showing me the character of those around me, especially Theo. You have soothed my broken heart and shown me what You were protecting me from. Thank You for your blessing of sending me Tamara as such a good friend. And Lord, whatever it is with Blake, I am enjoying being around him. I pray that Your will is shown in this situation, as it always is, but please continue to watch out for me, and I will take the path You show me, no matter where it leads. Amen."

I slipped back inside my room and pulled out a fresh pair of pajamas, when the sounds of crunching sent me back out to the balcony. I peered over the edge and made out a man walking with skis hanging over his shoulder. My heart leapt for a moment, thinking it was Blake, but then another man joined him and from the words I could hear, they were speaking German. What was I going to do if it was Blake, call out to him? That would make me look like a real psycho. I laughed that idea off and went back to bed.

*****

A few hours later I was on the slopes. My legs felt stiff from the cold and exertion of the last few days, especially my knees. Tara had been right about that.

I had yet to see Blake that morning. Because I crashed so early the night before, I hadn't run into him since the previous afternoon. During the morning lesson with the ski instructor, my eyes kept wandering over to the lodge door to see if he would walk out of it. Nothing happened for a while until finally, Theo walked out of the lodge. I assumed he'd been looking for Tara, but I didn't see her on the mountain that day where she usually was in the ski school zone. *None of my business what he's doing,* I reminded myself. The next time I looked over, Theo was standing at the base, and it appeared he was watching me. *Was he?* That would be so strange. I tried to carry on with the instruction as we were working on our form, but I suddenly felt the urge to be performative.

Something I always felt with Theo was the need to be perfect. Blake had shown me just the opposite, and in fact, had embraced my flaws. That was the difference between the men; though one I was dating, the other was just pretending. It was beginning to feel the opposite.

After several minutes with Theo watching my every move, Tara came expertly swooshing down the ski hill, laughing loudly. She was with another instructor, which I knew by their matching jackets. He took his goggles off, revealing himself to be young, blonde, and clean shaven with a stunning jawline. I guessed he was about Tara's age— mid-twenties. I could feel their chemistry from a distance. They looked like they went together, frankly— like they could be side by side in a clothing catalog.

Tara's laughter came to an abrupt stop when she noticed Theo, and she slowly skied over to him. She looked much stiffer than she had moments before, before she knew he was watching— like she'd just been caught doing something she shouldn't have been. But I felt for her because she didn't even know that Theo was watching her. I wondered if she'd rather been with the hunk she was skiing with, as she looked so happy and carefree.

I watched their awkward embrace as they shared a quick hug. It seemed cold, but then after talking for a moment, Theo and Tara started gliding over to the chair lift. So, he had been waiting for her all along, not watching me. It sure felt like he was, though.

Immersing myself back into the lesson, we were about to take a run when Blake tapped me on the shoulder. He joined me on the chairlift, and I was tickled to have another few minutes with him one on one.

"I didn't see you around last night. I ended up playing board games with members of your church until almost nine.

Dang, watch out for Cammy while playing Monopoly— I think she prints her own money."

"Oh? That's awesome you played with them. Yeah, I totally crashed last night. I fell asleep in my clothes, makeup, and everything. Woke up at 4 a.m. wondering what century I was living in."

"You must have needed it. I know I always sleep better in a cold environment. There's something so special about a snowy mountain range. I often think that God is a man of the mountains, too. I feel like I'm closer to Him when I'm higher in elevation."

I loved hearing Blake talk about God. He gave me something to think about as I had never considered the spiritual connection I felt there in Sage Mountain. "I've lived here my entire life and despite everything changing so rapidly the last few years, I can't see myself leaving. Even with no job and no idea how I'll cover my property taxes that have quadrupled, I must be addicted to the cold because nowhere else feels like home. I may have to leave, but where do you go from here?"

Blake pursed his lips together with bated breath, and I waited for his reply. "Colorado is pretty nice, if I say so myself." He grinned at me ear to ear.

"I have friends who moved down there, and they say the same, but there's no place like home. Besides, I'd be competing in a much larger market for jobs. I don't know if I have the competitive drive like city people. And I'm sure you can see; I don't handle rejection that great. But God has a plan for me, and I know He will guide me to the right place."

"That's right, Claire. What a relief it is to know that we aren't the ones in charge around here."

We both smiled, and the chair lift finally made it to the top, slowing down ever so slightly for us to disembark.

"Tips up!" The lift tech yelled from his booth, but it was already too late. Somehow my distraction got the better of me and my right ski caught on part of the platform, slowly tossing me from the chair onto the cold snow in front of me. A loud bell rang, alerting the fellow chair lift riders that there was an emergency, and the lift would be paused.

"You really know how to make an entrance, Claire." Blake helped me get up and out of the way of the lift before giving me a once over so he could see my face. "Nothing appears to be hurt externally, no bleeding, no black eyes. You may need a walker down the line, possibly both eyes replaced, but I think we can ski out of here today." He chuckled, and I groaned.

"Here we are again. Blake to my rescue," I smiled as he unclipped my skis and set them off to the side. "I'm okay— just internally scarred because this is so embarrassing." Peering over my shoulder, it didn't seem like anyone was looking my way, which was a relief.

"Don't worry about it. People are constantly wrecking as they get off the lift, go down the mountain… Once, a man fell down the stairs inside the lodge in his ski boots. He was totally fine— fell on his backside and just did the rumble down each step. Wow, did he have a good laugh after that one." He lifted his brows and shrugged.

I couldn't hold back my laughter. "You? You mean to tell me that you can be clumsy, too?"

He picked up a handful of snow and blew it in front of my face, each bit of it sparkling in the sunlight. "Occasionally, yes. But the real queen of clumsy is my mom. My father considered an ambulance being stationed outside their home just because it would make things more convenient. Her last injury was from trying to get up from a bar stool while realizing her feet were inside the rungs and somehow from there slid ten yards across the floor. We ran to the noise, only to find her under the Christmas tree."

"It sounds like I'll be in great company then."

Blake motioned for me to start down the hill in front of him, and I did, putting all of my techniques into motion. "Is there anything you suggest I do to improve?"

"You have some great fundamentals. I'm guessing you've taken some lessons over the course of your life? From here, you just need to relax and practice."

I let out a breath. Blake was so refreshing. He just wasn't a critical person and so nice to be around.

Right before I got to the halfway point, Theo cut me off on skis, forcing me to come to an abrupt stop.

"What in the world!?" I yelled out to Theo, who didn't stop.

Tara was close behind. I turned back to Blake, who was clapping.

"That was an incredible stop, Claire! And you didn't even fall. Your lessons are paying off."

Just then, my instructor, Trevor, appeared. "Sorry about that, Claire. I saw the whole thing; they know better than to go this fast in the beginners' area. I think Theo is miffed because Tara just dumped him."

My jaw dropped.

"But by the ease of that stop you just made, I think it's time we move over to the Blue runs. They are the next level in skiing. I can't take you, since the rest of the students aren't ready for that but— ",

Blake cut him off. "I can take her."

Trevor looked at Blake and then at me, eventually nodding his head.

"Okay, that works. Let me know how she does." Trevor gave Blake a fist bump and skied off to catch up with the rest of the teens who'd been skiing down the mountain while we spoke.

"Alright, then. You're under my power now." Blake did an impersonation of an evil laugh while I playfully smacked him in the arm. "Just kidding. I had a babysitter say that to me when I was little, and it traumatized me. I've considered therapy just to move past it. Anyway, let's head to the bottom. Do you feel ready to check out a Blue run? You definitely look ready, but it's your decision."

I appreciated Blake's pressure-free presence when it came to skiing. He was the polar opposite of Theo in every way. Ugh. I thought I needed a cattle prod to stop comparing Blake to Theo. "Maybe, yes. But first I want to master picking up a little more speed on the green runs!" I cheered, feeling a little anxiety in my voice, but also was ready to tackle a challenge. If anything, it would give me a story to tell Blake's parents that night.

"Great. Want to get a hot chocolate first or have it be our reward after?"

I liked the sound of that. "Reward. I'm very food motivated, like a retriever."

"The cutest retriever I've ever seen."

I blushed at his comment, not even sure if comparing me to a dog was a good thing, but I did it to myself. "Thank you?"

We both laughed at the conversation. We jumped on a chairlift and made our way back to the top. We ended up skiing the rest of the day, only breaking for a hot chocolate and warm pretzel. Blake brought one out with extra cheese for us to share.

"How did you know these giant pretzels are my favorite?" I demanded.

"It was a test. If you don't like pretzels, I'm not sure I can continue this fake relationship." He dunked a buttery piece into cheese and popped it into his mouth. We finished our snack and put our gloves back on.

"What time is it?" I asked.

"I think it's quarter to four, so only time for one more run if you have it in you. If we continue this pace, you'll be on Black Diamonds tomorrow. By next week, I won't be able to keep up. By next year, the Olympics."

I gave him a smirk and rolled my eyes. I knew the latter of that statement was fluff, but I was curious what he thought. The second we sat down on the chairlift, I turned to him. "Do you think I have what it takes to be a skier?"

He gave me a confused look. "Claire… I don't know what people have said to you in your life. It's pretty clear you've been treated like you're unworthy of love from that jerk ex of yours… And I know what it's like to be living in the shadow of your father. But one thing I know for certain: You *are* a skier. Your level of ability does not change that fact; whether or not you participate does. And you have made such great progress just in the last two days. What you needed was the chance to show yourself what you can do."

His words hit me like a brick as we stepped off the chairlift. "Blake, thank you for being here for me. I hope we can remain friends after this because your light and positivity are just what I needed in my life. You are heaven sent. We better get back so I can check in with my group and get ready for tonight."

I gave him a short hug, and he told me he would be heading to his parents early, and that he'd see me there. I gave a thumbs up and took off down my favorite green run of the day, "Powder Puff."

My group was nowhere to be found in the lodge. I remembered Tamara had booked a pedicure for the afternoon, and I could see Mickey riding the magic carpet lift with Trevor. I was sure there was a story there, but I'd have to hear what it was later. Back in my hotel room, I took a quick shower, styled my hair in a beach wave, and put on my new outfit. Everything fit perfect, and Tamara's boots were just tall

enough that they made my calves look chiseled. I snapped a
picture in the full-length closet mirror and sent it to Tamara.

**Thank you again for the boots. Will let you know
when I'm back. Will be on Blueberry Basin, at the
James Walker residence. And if I go missing, for my
crime documentary, there is no need to embellish
the facts. I did NOT light up a room xx**

Tamara sent me some laughing emojis and a heart.
She was exhausted and had been battling some pretty severe
nausea, but we promised to get together when that passed. I
was set to go then, grabbed my small purse with my phone,
lip gloss and some breath mints just in case we ate anything
really fragrant, and went to the downstairs lobby for the car.

A sleek, black suburban with tinted windows silently
came to a stop outside the front doors. While I had no idea
who it was for, Blake did say he was sending a *car,* not a
behemoth of the road. When the valet came inside, calling for
"Claire Riley," I followed him to the car where he opened the
back seat door for me. The interior lit up, and a smooth-faced
driver who wore a suit looked back at me.

"Good evening, Miss. I am Tom, your driver tonight. We will be at Mr. Walker's residence shortly."

"Thank you, Tom." I'd never been to one of the homes, er— mansions, on the mountain. They started popping up right after our town was bought by James Walker, and my gut told me his house was the first to go up. Tom wasn't the chatty type, judging by his lack of words to me, and that was fine. It had been a long day of skiing, and my body was tired. The smoothness of the car driving through the crunchy snow was lulling me to sleep, but the moment I closed my eyes, we came to a stop. Tom turned off the car, got out, and immediately opened my door in one fluid movement.

"Ms. Riley, right this way."

He held out his hand for me to take as I got out of the car. The heated driveway and sidewalks were immaculately free from snow and illuminated by gleaming solar lights. The house had dark siding and a black roof with brown trim that matched the pavers on the sidewalks. The front side had a few windows, revealing a glow from within. Aesthetically, it was a stylishly designed house and made me remember just how much I enjoyed being a designer. For that night, I would put the nagging realization of needing to find another job away but come next week when the fun fantasy was over, I would hit the job search.

The front door swung open. "Claire! You made it." Blake stood at the entryway, wearing a gray button up shirt tucked into dark jeans, a blue sweater, and loafers. He looked boyish dressed up, and I liked it. "You look lovely. Come on in. My parents are dying to meet you." Holding out his hand, I took it and walked inside.

"Thank you, Tom." I looked back, and he gave me a nod, returning to his vehicle.

Blake walked me inside and my jaw dropped. The backside of the house was completely glass. It was a stunning view of Blueberry Basin, which included Pryors Peak, the resort's biggest mountain. The location was impeccable; his father had excellent taste.

"You must be Claire!" A woman walked into the living room and shook my hand.

"Claire, this is my mother, Patsy. And my dad, James!"

Mr. Walker himself came barreling into the room, profusely apologizing for his tardiness. "I'm sorry, I had to take a call. So nice to meet you, Claire. Blake has been talking about his new girlfriend for the last two hours. It's lovely to put a face to the name."

He told them I was his girlfriend? I knew we were fake dating for the sake of my own needs, but I was shocked that he would continue the ruse with his parents. That had much longer implications than anything else. I hadn't even told anyone that we were dating but just let the rumors fly. This seemed to change the tables. After I was able to swallow that pill, I turned to James and took in the man who had inadvertently gotten me fired from my job.

"Wonderful to meet you both. What a gorgeous home you have here. You have excellent taste in location."

"Thank you, dear. Blake tells us that you were born and raised here? I bet you've seen quite a lot of changes in your lifetime."

I held back my laughter. He didn't know the first of it. "Oh yes. This place used to be a small community of miners and the railroad. The mountains were skiable of course but on just a much smaller scale. As you know, we only had a rope tow. Now there's heated bubble chairs and the little lifts even have bars to keep people from falling. That was quite the change."

"But that didn't stop Claire from falling out today, did it?" Blake busted up laughing, taking a sip of his hot tea.

"Claire, may I get you something to drink?" Patsy asked. "We're warming up with Moroccan mint tea this evening."

"That sounds lovely, thank you."

Patsy clasped her hands together and smiled, departing for the kitchen.

"Dad, Claire actually worked on the Sage Mountain Airport design."

Though I was considering sharing that fact myself, since the words were out, they felt in bad taste.

"Is that so? What do you do, Claire?"

"I'm a designer, mostly creating unique indoor spaces these days. I created the airport lounge."

He lit up like a Christmas tree. "We loved that design and are very excited to bring it into fruition. May I ask, why did you turn down the job for the outdoor area?"

I felt a scowl move across my face as my jaw went slack. "I didn't turn it down. I submitted a design, and then I was fired for it." The air in the room became thick and uncomfortable. I may have overshared, but the confusion was real.

James gathered his thoughts; his brow furrowed. "We never received your design, Claire. Who oversaw the project?"

He was asking for names? Yikes… Not that it would have been hard for him to find out for himself, so I might as well have said. "Patricia."

James was mid-sip of his steaming hot tea when I answered. He nearly choked in response. "Patricia has been on the outs for almost a year after getting tangled up in a scheme to embezzle money from the firm. She's only still an employee because HR couldn't prove she was directly involved. Claire, Patricia is a very unhappy person that we need to pray for, but so you're aware, she never submitted a design on your behalf. In fact, she told us last Friday that the designer we were looking forward to hearing from declined the job and *quit.*"

Blake put his hand on my shoulder as I took it all in. The betrayal was real, but something James said stuck out to me the most: *We need to pray for Patricia.* That thought could not have been further from my mind every time I dealt with her, and it was a humbling thought. *Lord, I pray for those who have hurt me.*

"Who's hungry?" Patsy walked over from the kitchen holding a charming teacup and saucer with an intoxicating mint aroma.

James was the first to answer. "I'm so hungry that I may waste away." He put a hand on his portly stomach and followed his wife into the dining area. Blake and I just a stepped behind.

While the home was an open concept, the dining area had a short wall that divided it from the kitchen. Once I turned the corner, I saw the long, gorgeous dark wood table perfectly set with a dramatic silver table runner. Each porcelain plate had a modest silver rim and sat on a black charger plate. Three candles ran down the center of the table, each bright white, held by classic sterling silver candlesticks. The Walkers had impeccable taste for tableware, décor, and homes.

Patsy lifted up the lids to the dishes in the center of the table, revealing a roast, colorful vegetables, and a delectable salad with creamy dressing. "I hope you're hungry," Patsy spoke to the room but directed her attention to me. "Dig in, Claire. You're a guest, so you go first."

I reached for the serving ware, my hand feeling foreign on the heavy material, and I felt self-conscious serving myself in front of people watching. Taking the salad plate, I doled out a healthy portion of what looked like a Caesar onto it. I was ready to sit back down and just eat that, but Patsy piped up before I did. "James has already carved the roast."

"Thank you." I took the metal tongs and retrieved the smallest piece from the side, placing it on my dinner plate along with a hearty scoop of vegetables. "It smells amazing, Patsy. Thank you for this meal," I said as I set my plate down and waited for the others to get their portions.

After everyone had food, I didn't want to be the one who took the first bite, so I waited. Blake was the first, so I dug in. While the food was divine, the company was even more so. I was pleasantly surprised by Blake's parents' sense of humor and the lighthearted conversations and funny anecdotes that James shared. When Patsy stepped away at the end, returning with a tray holding four perfectly plated desserts, I was glad the evening wasn't over yet. "Cheesecake, anyone?" My favorite.

After dessert, James pulled out a cigar from his shirt pocket, under his unbuttoned jacket. "I know, bad habit. Blake, my boy, why don't you join me and tell me your plans for New Year's Eve tomorrow."

Blake wiped his mouth with the silky napkin and slid out of his chair but didn't leave the room without kissing me on the forehead. Though it wasn't on the lips, it was the first time he kissed me. I was shocked. We never said we would do any overt displays of affection. But then again, even if we had, the rules were changing every moment.

I watched him walk out of the room as I regained my composure. No need to let Patsy think that was unusual or unexpected. "Shall we go sit by the fire, Claire?"

I nodded, and we found a place to sit on the overstuffed leather sectional. It wasn't as stiff as it looked and actually quite comfortable. As I looked around the room, I loved everything in it, especially the stone fireplace that went all the way to the ceiling— eighteen feet, if I had to guess.

"It's so nice to meet you, Claire. You're the first girl whom Blake has brought home, you know." Patsy winked at me. "I take it that things are very special between you two."

Her words were a double whammy. I looked over to the glass doors to see Blake and his father stargazing, the smoke from James' cigar billowing above him.

"He is a really special guy." It was true, Blake was a gem. He just wasn't mine, though I was starting to wish he was.

"It comes at a great time. James is ready to retire, but he doesn't want to hand the reins over to Blake until he's married. Call him old-fashioned? James is worried that our handsome boy will be thought of as a playboy unless he's settled down with a family. But no pressure from us; go at your own pace."

Patsy was beaming as my stomach felt like it fell three stories. It all made sense now. This is why Blake introduced me as his girlfriend; the optics of the public forehead kiss; the humble bragging about my work. Blake needed me to be his fake girlfriend just as much as I needed him.

And I had thought he was falling for me. No. He was priming me for the big one.

As James and Blake shuffled back in from the patio, everything was different. It was like someone had removed the rose-colored lenses from my eyes. I put my best face forward, helping Blake out by being the best fake girlfriend there ever was. When he made a joke, I laughed. When he spoke about his favorite pets at the animal shelter, I put my hand on his. And when the night came to a natural close, I stood up, expressing it was past my bedtime. Everyone gave me a hug goodnight, and Blake walked me out. I didn't realize it before, but Tom had been waiting outside this entire time.

"Thank you for coming, Claire. It was the perfect evening." Blake had his arm around me as we walked outside. He grabbed a heavy coat from the rack and slid it over my shoulders.

"I had a lovely evening."

Once the door shut behind us, I got real. "I hope that helped you out. Your mom told me about your dad not wanting to leave the company to you until you had a wife." The color from Blake's face drained. "It's totally cool. I just wish you had told me before, that's all. I'm glad we could help each other out like this."

"Claire, believe me when I say things are not what they seem with— "

I cut him off, feeling my knees shake in the cold. "Blake, it's all good. I promise. At first, yes, I was caught by surprise, but we each had something to gain from this, and

I'm happy to help. Now, I really should go before I get frostbite."

My teeth were chattering as I walked towards the Suburban with Tom springing into action to open the door for me. After Tom returned to the driver's seat, I told him to wait just a moment, and I rolled down the window, handing Blake his jacket. "Here's your coat. And before I forget… Tomorrow is the last day of the ski retreat, and I have a huge week ahead of me for my job search, so I'll probably hit the road after my ski lesson. It was great meeting you, Blake. I wish you all the best in the world. You really do deserve it."

I rolled the window back up and fought back my emotions. I thought Blake and I were toeing the line, forming a true connection, but instead, it was just what we said it was: a fake relationship. I clasped my hands and said a silent prayer.

Lord, you know my heart. You know my needs before I do. I trust that You will lead me down the right path. Amen.

Feeling sad wasn't on my bingo card for that night, but it was my own fault. I looked into something deeper and felt things that weren't real. I was paying the price. Again. Maybe it was time I swore off love forever.

Returning back to the lodge, I texted Tamara that I was ready for bed. I filled it with many more platitudes about the beautiful home, the magical views, and the delicious food. I left out the parts about his father telling me the truth about my old boss, and his mother revealing family secrets, and the fact that Blake had never brought a girl home before me. What did it all mean? And my mind went back to Patricia never submitting my design. Did she really dislike me that much? What in the world was going on there? I'd get to the bottom of that later. I just had to get some much-needed rest before my last ski day.

Chapter 9

December 31st

Of all the days to sleep in, it was the perfect one to do so. I felt no hurry to get out of bed and face reality. The bed in my hotel room was luxurious with soft down pillows and duvet, topped with thick cotton sheets. For being a busy ski lodge, it was very quiet there, more so than my condo in the heart of town. I slept like a rock, and I woke up with a feeling of clarity.

Blake wasn't out to hurt me. Blake was out to help me, and in return, help himself. I couldn't be mad at that since he held up his end of the bargain. I just wished I'd known what my end was… But would it have changed anything? Would I have turned it down if it wasn't completely one sided, in my favor? No, I supposed not.

As I brushed my teeth and combed my hair, I wondered why Blake hadn't brought anyone home over the years. He was gorgeous, at least to me. His appealing auburn hair and olive skin were so striking with his pale eyes. He had a wonderful personality and always kept me laughing. He told me right off the bat that his goal was to have a wife and children one day, so… What was the hold up? Surely a guy like him could have had any woman he wanted. I got dressed, focused on the topic like a laser, sighing. It was really none of my business, I supposed.

It was a rash decision that I would leave that night instead of the next morning, and I was regretting it, but I felt like I should get back. I had left so hastily the prior week after getting fired, that my condo was a complete disaster inside. If I could get it nice and clean, my clothes washed and dishes done, I could start the new year with peace and better intentions. On that note, I pulled out my devotional book and Bible.

After being immersed in the text for nearly half an hour, my stomach growled. I felt so much better after getting connected with God at the start of my day. Next, it was time to connect with pancakes and syrup.

The dining room had all but cleared out by the time I arrived. Only a few stragglers were still eating. I couldn't see who the groups of people were in the booths that lined both walls, so I beelined it for the front booth. That way, I wouldn't have to walk past anyone.

Once I devoured my plate of pancakes and slurped down an extra-strong coffee, I got up and gathered my hat and gloves. I was on my last ski outfit of the trip, wearing a pink zip up pullover under my bright red jacket. The colors had worked so well with Tara when she looked like a walking Valentine, so I decided to try it myself. That, and I really needed to do some laundry.

As soon as I turned around, Theo was standing in front of me. "Oh, hello," I said quietly, almost under my breath and walked around him. He stayed in place, stoic, but ended up finding me a few minutes later in the gear room. I was at the gear counter, asking for a ski boot a size larger when he interjected.

"Why would you get a bigger boot?" He looked at me with confusion.

Why was it any of his business what I did or wore?

"Because my feet felt pinched; not that it makes any difference to you, Theo."

He nodded, and the social cues implied he should walk away, but he stayed.

"Can I help you with something, man?" The guy at the counter directed his question to Theo, helping me out because it was awkward with him standing there.

"No, I'm good. Thanks."

I felt my eyes get big. I'd never heard him say "thanks" to anyone. He just wasn't one for platitudes, was all.

"Claire, could I talk to you?"

I held my breath. What could he want? Did he want to apologize for emotionally cheating on me with Tara? Or ask me if I could pretend to be his fake girlfriend to make her jealous? This was Theo after all, so I was sure I would be surprised, regardless.

"I don't think so, Theo. There's nothing to say." I kept my eyes on the guy behind the counter, as he quickly adjusted my bindings to pair with the slightly larger boot.

"Alright. If you change your mind, I'll be outside."

I almost let out a joke, asking, "Is that a threat," but I didn't want to extend the conversation. I very recently had hoped that he would have proposed to me, but after meeting Blake, I learned what a connection felt like, so I wanted nothing short of that.

Once I made it outside, I felt relief that Theo was not waiting for me. Instead, I saw Tara watching a group of teens do the "French Fries" position. I was heading towards the lift, knowing I was too late for the first lesson to jump in when she called my name.

"Claire! Wait a minute, please." She motioned for the other instructor who had been standing there to keep an eye on the teens, and she expertly glided over to me. "Can we talk for a minute?" Her eyes looked bright, and there was a sense of urgency in her voice.

"Okay, sure. What's up?"

"I just wanted to let you know that I broke up with Theo. And there's something I want to tell you: I swear I didn't know that you and he were still dating when he and I met. If I had known anything of the like, I wouldn't have pursued anything with that guy." She looked like she had tears in her eyes as she spoke to me. "Please forgive me, Claire. I am not that type of woman." A tear fell from her cheek.

I leaned in and hugged her. "I know you didn't know. He played both of us, and there's nothing to forgive."

The relief on her face was instant as she let out a breath and released her shoulders. "That is so good to hear, Claire. Thank you. Anyway, it's good that it's all out in the open, so we never waste our time on a guy like that again. Not that you need to worry about that. You've found yourself such a hunk with that Blake guy!"

I couldn't keep the ruse any longer. I had to come clean. "He's not really my boyfriend. Once I came here and saw that Theo was here, I needed a quick solution to save face. And then after I found out that he'd been cheating on me…"

Tara put her hand on my shoulder and shook her head.

"I kind of had a freakout. Blake proposed the idea to be my fake boyfriend for the week. That's all it is. The relationship isn't real whatsoever." Shrugging my shoulders, I saw Tara's gaze avert from my own, looking just past me.

"Are you sure about that?" She smiled, giving me a quick hug, and went back to her lesson. I slowly turned around to see Blake. He wasn't wearing ski clothes, but instead, a pea coat over a wool weather, and a scarf hanging around his neck. He walked over to me and held out a hot drink, as he had two in his hands.

"Blake? What are you doing?" I had more questions than answers. Was he not skiing today? Was this our final goodbye? Had I left behind a shoe at his parents' home last night?

"I was hoping we could catch up for a few minutes if you had them to spare?" He looked over at the chair lift. The line looked a mile long.

"Yes, I guess I do. That will take forever." I opened the lid on the drink and looked inside. It was a towering hot chocolate with hundreds of marshmallows, just how I liked it.

"Great. First, I just want to address a few things that may have been misconstrued. Starting with what my mom told you. Yes, it is all true about my father not wanting to hand me the company until I get married." His addressing this piece of information made me feel validated that yes, it was newsworthy and surprising. He continued, "That being said, I don't want the company."

What? My jaw went completely slack. "Why not? It's one of the most powerful corporations in America. You'd literally *own snow.*"

He shook his head. "It's not who I am. And believe me, I've tried to be that guy. I've done everything I could to be that guy. But I just can't. It's not where my priorities lie."

My reaction was mostly visceral.

"It's not that I can't do the job; I am capable. It goes deeper than that. It's not even about me; it's about my father. He has this huge legacy that I feel I'll be compared to for the rest of my life, and it's crippling. Comparison really is the thief of joy, like they say. I want to forge my own path, find my own thing. That's why I've held back from dating for so long; why I haven't found a wife, because I knew he would hand it over to me the moment I did. Meanwhile, I'm still trying to figure it all out."

Things were starting to make sense. And boy, did I relate to his feelings. Though we came from two different walks of life, we had the same experiences through different lenses. I could see that God put Blake in my life just when I needed him. I was learning so much from that man.

"There are two other things I want to tell you, and I'll get out of your hair. First, my father made a call to Patricia after you left last night, and he got a copy of the plan you made for the outdoor space for the airport. He loved it, especially the cigar bar, given his personal preference for the indulgence."

Blake smiled for the first time in our conversation as my heart leapt at where this was leading.

"Apparently, Patricia has been on thin ice for a while since getting wrapped up in some funny business. She thought the design could save her standing, so she was planning on submitting it next week while taking the credit completely."

I shook my head. It sounded like she'd been in a very desperate situation, one I wouldn't wish on anyone.

"My father will be implementing the outdoor space to your design, and he's personally sent you an email regarding a job offer for a new position."

Wow. I was floored but had a feeling why he would be showing me such kindness. "That's wonderful, Blake. But he only did that because he thinks I'm your girlfriend."

Blake's smile faded. "Actually, no. I told them the truth last night, that we weren't dating. They were disappointed in me, but it led to the first real conversation we've had in years about where I see my life taking me. Thanks to you, Claire, because for the first time in years, I feel like I have a real future on my own terms. Lord willing, of course. And I want you to know that my father wanted your design whether or not we were in a relationship. The design really is perfect, Claire. Nothing else will ever hold a candle."

"Well, it's safe to say I didn't see this coming today. Thank you, Blake. You helped me out tremendously." I looked over my shoulder, not wanting to leave the conversation, but feeling it come to a natural close. The line had dwindled down to just a few people. By the time I got there, it would be my turn to get on the lift. "I guess this is it. Take care of yourself, okay?" I leaned in and gave him a one-armed hug, holding my tall hot chocolate to the side so I wouldn't spill it. I planned to drink it on the lift up.

"Claire?"

"Yes, Blake?

"Since you don't have to worry about the job search, that is, if the job proposal works for you, I was wondering if you'd consider staying one more night. It's New Year's Eve after all, and I was hoping you would be my date."

"I don't know, Blake. I don't think the lodge is doing anything special tonight."

"They are doing an early fireworks display at ten tonight, perfect for all of us who can't stay awake until midnight."

He smiled, his eyes sparkling. I couldn't say no to that.

"If you decide to stay, meet me at nine by the fireplace. If you decide to go home, I understand. I hope to see you, Claire." He turned and left, disappearing into the lodge.

*****

The relief of my job released the tension throughout my back that I didn't even realize I'd been carrying that week. And Blake's asking me out intrigued me. I could barely wipe the smile off of my face as I tried to gracefully glide over to the ski lift, but it was more of a flailing than anything. By the time I got there, no one was in line. Tucking my poles under the arm that held my hot chocolate, I reached out for the chair with the other. Lo and behold, Theo came tearing it up from behind, taking the seat beside me. Ugh.

"Really, Theo?" This was getting weird. "How can I help you?" I didn't mean to sound as snarky as I did, but it didn't faze him either way.

"I need to talk to you, Claire."

I looked over his shoulder. He had to have been close to take this opportunity. Had he been watching me this whole time? Watching Blake and me, too? "Well, I'm stuck with you on this lift for at least five minutes, so go ahead." I took a drink of my hot chocolate that was perfectly cooled off, so I took a few more, knowing I would have to drink it before we made it to the top.

"I wanted to know if… If I could have another chance?"

My eyes almost bugged out of my head. "No." The firm rejection was all I could muster. I felt my body revolt at the thought. "You were talking to another woman while we were together. You dumped me the night before my big thirtieth birthday. You didn't care that I didn't want to break up. I spent Christmas alone. I didn't hear from you for two weeks and… Now you want me back?" I left out the part where he made me feel terrible, because I didn't want to go there.

"I know, and…"

The next words out of his mouth were so hard for him to say. I didn't think he'd expected to be using the phrase at that moment, but the situation was spiraling out of control.

"I'm sorry, Claire…" His voice trailed off, and I couldn't tell if he was apologizing or asking me if he should be sorry.

"Is that a question or an apology? Don't answer that. It doesn't matter, Theo."

He smiled, and I didn't know why.

"Great! So, can we start over? Truth is, I didn't realize what I had walked away from until I saw you here this week. I think with a full season of ski lessons, every weekend at least, we could have you in a good place— if not this year, then next. What do you think?"

I looked at him in horror before bursting into laughter. "No, Theo. I do not want to start over. I do not want to commit the rest of my life to something that I'm really experiencing now for the first time, only because I'm free to do so on my own terms. I do not want to be in a relationship with you. We weren't really in love. You didn't love me."

Next, it was Theo who looked confused.

Suddenly, the ski lift came to a screeching halt, as a small alarm could be heard from the top. "Oh no. Did someone fall?" I wondered aloud.

"I hope not. It gets cold fast when we stay still." He extended his arm like he was going to wrap it around me when I used the bar on my lap to scoot further away from him. After a moment of silence, he laughed. We were only halfway up the lift, completely stuck with one another when I prayed for Theo.

Lord, please give me the words to say to this person. He isn't seeing things clearly, and I pray that I can get through to him and get through this.

"I forgive you." The words flew out of my mouth before I could think about them, before I could even feel them out to see if it was true. But then I knew; I did forgive him. "And… I have moved on in life. And so have you, or at least, you did. You didn't love me, Theo. You loved the idea of me, and I see now just how mutual that was. I did the same thing to you, and for that, I'm sorry."

"Claire, I do love you. I am in love with you. Tara was just a skier who liked me and yes, I took it too far. I shouldn't have entertained a friendship with her while we were together. But it's you, Claire. It's always been you."

He was pleading with me, and three weeks ago, I would've cried happy tears for this very moment. This was the man I always wanted him to show. But it became clear: He just wanted what he couldn't have. I thought of Blake; he never made me feel like I was inadequate. I thought back to Theo's skiing lessons comment with dread. The chair lift was just moments away from the top if it would ever start going again. I turned and looked Theo in the eyes, holding his gaze. There was a sad person inside, and I didn't know how that happened, but it was not my fault that he was that way. I'd shown him nothing but grace and kindness. The buck stopped there.

Before I could open my mouth and have a rebuttal, he put his head in his hands. "Have I ever told you what it was like to lose my parents at such a young age?"

The mix of surprise and cold made my face go numb. I shook my head, mumbling a reply.

"It was so brutal. The world felt empty. I've never experienced a loss like that since… until now."

My eyes felt like they could bulge out of my head. Theo wasn't one for the dramatics, so I was genuinely shocked he felt that way. Looking back, I didn't know our relationship was strong enough to warrant feelings like that to begin with. "Theo, I am honored that you feel that way about me but…" As I trailed off, praying for the right words to say, he interjected.

"I made a colossal mistake, Claire. I didn't know what I had until I left you. And I'm sorry for being such a jerk about the skiing thing. Honestly, just seeing you here on skis makes my heart full. I've never wanted anything more than this version of you, Claire. But I do hear what you're saying, even though it's hard, and if you tell me you never want to ski again, I can live with it. I can make that sacrifice, because being with you is better than skiing. We can get married tomorrow if you want. If you take me back, I will get down on one knee and make it official the second we get off this chair. Please consider it. I will do anything to make this right with you."

The chair lift jolted somewhere in his plea, and we started creeping to the top once again while a few cheers were heard behind us. The man who I loved and wanted to marry was offering the chance. We were finally aligned in seeing the version of each other that we always wanted to be with. I could ski away from this lift as an engaged woman. I would be Mrs. Riley McCain with the perfect ski-jumper fiancé to impress my famous downhill skier dad. It was everything I ever wanted. And I meant, *was.*

The chair slowed, and I slid off onto the snow with him coming up behind me. "I can't give you what you're looking for. While I would have done anything to hear those words three weeks ago, this week here has shown me that while I was searching for a relationship that made me feel worthy, I found that kind of fulfillment only comes from Jesus. And learning how to ski– accomplishing something– I feel whole for the first time in my life. Happy… that I am enough. I see now that being with you was something I wanted to do because you made me feel better about my life, but I don't need a relationship to feel whole. I hope you find what you're looking for. But I want you to know, it's going to start with forming a personal relationship with God."

I stood there as I watched the man I had loved and was saying goodbye to silently listen to my words. I knew he was in pain; it was hard to feel the way he did, chasing perfection all the time within himself and others. No one would ever be able to match up to his standards. I reached my hands out to him, touching his arms. "No one can love you the way that God can. And it is with His love that you can learn to love others. Goodbye, Theo."

I slid off, going twenty yards to the left, the top of where two runs met. I watched as he waited several seconds before he turned the other direction and went down a Double Black Diamond.

Lord, please let that seed bear fruit.

There I stood at a crossroads. I could have taken the easy route and may never have had to use my strength or ability. Nothing would have hurt my knees, and I wouldn't have to worry about feeling embarrassed or sad because I likely wouldn't fall or get hurt. If I took the hard route, I might have gotten hung up on steep terrain. Other skiers might have cut me off and scared me. It could have taken me three times longer to navigate and falling was almost inevitable. I could guarantee that my entire body would ache with pain from the exertion, and a show of strength and bravery would have been mandatory.

The easy Green run to the right was called "Pinyons Path." It was smooth and groomed and led to my favorite parts of the resort, which I felt very comfortable on. The Blue run to the left was called "Keith's Kicker," and it lived up to that phrase. It was named after an infamous skier who frequented there in the 70s and who made that run himself when it was just an off-piste beater full of rocks and obstacles.

I closed my eyes. "God, I pray for less of me— my insecurities, fears and hangups. And I pray for more of You in my life. Your blessings, love, and guidance. You are the ski patroller of my life, Lord, and You'll keep my paths straight."

I tipped my skis down and went to the left. It was harder than I could have ever imagined. The downhill decline was frightening. If it didn't say Blue level, I would have thought I'd completed the hardest run the resort had. It felt like hours that I was up there, and I wanted to give up. I wanted to unclip my skis and walk down with one in each hand. There would have been no shame in that, but I was out there to prove something to no one but myself, and to God, that I could trust Him for leading me there. I had been equipped with the lessons that taught me the skills to do that. It was time to remind the little girl inside of me that I could still chase dreams that seemed far-fetched. It was never too late to start.

My knees felt like they were going to break by the time I got to the end, as they'd been in the "Pizza" triangle formation nearly all the way down. I must've looked like I was riding an invisible horse with how wide my legs were, and my posture was that of a man from Notre Dame. But it didn't matter; I made it down an extremely challenging ski run by myself. Not only did I stay upright the entire time, but I didn't get near the trees, rocks, or other obstacles that may have sent me into a tailspin. At the bottom of the run, I turned to look back at what I'd accomplished. It looked impossibly steep, and in the shadow of the mountain, it was icy. A smile came creeping across my face, while the sharp shaving noises from the other skiers edging their way down felt like music to my ears. I felt complete. *Thank you, Lord. I am a skier.*

Chapter 10

December 31st

Turning in my ski gear, I slipped into the pair of slippers I'd worn to the gear room that morning, feeling my foot return to full mobility. The stairs brought out more aches and pains in my knees, but I welcomed them, for the payoff was greater than anything else.

Returning to my room, I took a hot shower, thinking of picking up take-out dinner on my way home. I was going over all of the places in my head to see what I had a craving for. Thai? Pizza? A steak salad from my neighborhood bar & grill? Nothing sounded good. I wasn't sure what I was in the mood for.

Since meals were covered there, I thought maybe I should just grab a bite downstairs and be responsible about things. I could go to the grocery store first thing the morning and restock my fridge with only the healthiest items. Being an adult could be so boring.

I got dressed and dried my hair, putting everything else into my suitcase except my phone. My curiosity was killing me, so I checked my email to see if Blake's father had in fact sent a job offer. Lo and behold, sitting at the top of my inbox was a message from James Walker.

The job offer was out of this world. From the looks of it, I would be the *Senior Design Consultant* for the entire company. I wouldn't be designing each space from scratch, but more so helping others create the vision I had— delegating, finalizing, approving— what Patricia's job should have been for me, had she not gotten wrapped up in the wrong things. With excitement, I read and loved everything about the job. I nearly lost consciousness when I read the salary was 50% higher than what I had been making, plus *four weeks* of vacation time, cleverly called "PTO— Powder Time-Off." It *was* a skiing conglomerate, after all... The start date he listed was two weeks from that day and the proverbial cherry on top. "God, you really are made of miracles." This was better than I could have ever imagined. I replied to his message immediately.

> Thank you, Mr. Walker, for your job offer. I accept your proposal, and I look forward to working with you.
> Regards,
> Claire Riley

What in the world would I do with two weeks off of work? As I put my phone into my purse, I looked out the window. Maybe I would come back there for a weekend on my own. Maybe I would take Anna's advice and get a change of scenery. I looked forward to telling her all that had transpired in my life since our last appointment.

After getting my things packed up, I rolled my suitcase to sit by the door. I did one last look around the room and was pleased that I found a hair scrunchy that I nearly left behind. My phone buzzed from my purse, and upon retrieving it, I saw a text from my mother reminding me that they were leaving Alaska the next day and would be out of pocket while traveling. I took the cue and without thinking, dialed her number. She answered on the second ring.

"Hi, Mom."

"Well, hello, Claire! How is my favorite daughter today?"

My mother's cheery voice made me feel guilty for not calling more, though we did exchange texts frequently, except for this week. "I'm good, how are you?" My voice cracked as I felt my emotions betraying me. Why was I feeling upset again?

"Oh no, Claire. What's wrong?" I could hear her television turn off in the background. "Let me put you on speakerphone. Your father is here, too."

"Nothing… I'm feeling better now, actually. Today was a weird day, is all. It's just good to hear your voice." I felt like I was back home whenever we spoke. That day *was* a bizarre day with Theo asking for another chance. There might have been a little more to it than that, like how, despite all of my progress, I felt like I was getting roped back into his manipulation and that scared me… But I really didn't want to bring my parents down with my failures.

"Nothing that Theo can't help with, I'm sure?" My mother was smiling as she spoke, I could tell.

"Actually..." I took a breath, thinking she had to see this coming. "We broke up." I couldn't have felt any stupider as I did right at that moment, but then my mother was exclaiming something to my father and said she was going to hand the phone off to him.

"Claire?"

I smacked the phone on my forehead, feeling overwhelmed. "Hi, Dad. Alaska sounds fun." It was all I could muster up as my voice was betraying me once again.

"What's this I hear about Theo?"

I knew it, he was disappointed in me again. I felt bad for him for disappointing him so much. "Yeah, it didn't work out." I sniffled again, but this time it was happy tears. "It's for the best. We want different things."

"Well, Claire. That certainly is a surprise."

I knew it. That crushed him. "I'm so sorry, dad." The tears came flowing, and I choked out my words.

"Claire, don't cry. I don't want to sound insensitive here, but I'm SO glad to hear you two are done. Your mother and I thought he was a pompous, egotistical jerk from the moment we met him."

My jaw dropped to the floor. "You did? I thought... I thought you liked him— I mean, he's just so into skiing and…"

"I only thought *you* liked him, Claire. We may not have seen what you saw in him, but we just want you to be happy."

My tears turned to joy. "Thank you, Dad. You don't know how much that means to me."

"Claire, I know I've made some mistakes in my life, and I wish I had you when I was younger, so I could relate to you better. But believe me when I say you are the biggest accomplishment of my life. I couldn't be prouder of my daughter."

I felt years of self-inflicted pain become undone. "There's something else I wanted to tell you." I remembered what Blake told me earlier, how I *was* a skier because I was there. My ability didn't define the status of my participation. "I have taken up skiing, for real this time."

My father gasped on the other end of the line. "Really? That's great, kiddo. But..." There was a hesitancy in his voice, "Do you enjoy it?"

I was starting to realize just how well he knew me. "Yes, well… I think so. Sort of?" We both laughed. "It feels great to accomplish something. And I'm happy to tell you that I did the 'Keith's Kicker' run in solo today. Didn't fall or mess up once."

"Claire! That's a challenging *Blue* run! How fantastic. I'm so proud of you." My mother echoed his sentiments in the background. "When you were little, maybe two or three years old, you hated the snow. When your mother tried to get you into your snowsuit, you asked to go swimming instead. I never pushed the snow on you because it's not for everyone, Claire. And I always thought it was okay if it wasn't your thing. But it sounds like you've conquered this, too, just like everything else you set your mind to."

It was true, I really did hate the snow as a kid. But it had become like I didn't know anything else. I thought about my week with Blake and smiled. "I will tell you what I really enjoy about skiing. There's a thrill of catching speed while knowing you are in control of your skis; the joy of the gorgeous views, especially on bluebird days with not a cloud in the sky; the hot chocolate in the lodge is universally hot and amazing; and, the new cute guy I met doesn't hurt, either."

I could hear both my parents laughing on the other end of the phone, my mother clapping. "Do tell us the details, Claire! What's his name?"

"His name is Blake Walker. And he's the kindest man I've ever known." Saying it out loud rang the bell of my heart. What was I doing? Why was I about to walk away from the perfect man for me? Theo had rattled me, making me think I wasn't ready for something real, but God was greater than that.

My parents loved every moment as I caught them up on Blake, while I realized that all of the reasons for keeping things from them no longer made sense.

"So, what's next with Blake? Will you be seeing him again soon?" my mother asked, and I could hear my father agree with the question.

"He's asked me to join him for fireworks tonight here at the Superstition Mountain Lodge." I realized then just how much I wanted to go.

"We hope you have a wonderful time, Claire. And we can't wait to meet Blake. We are so, so proud of everything you've been doing to work on yourself and enjoy new experiences. When we get back, you and I will have to take some runs together at Sage Mountain. What do you think, Claire?"

My father asked the question I'd been waiting for my entire life. Turned out, I had to be the one who took the first step rather than waiting on everyone else to take it for me. Anna, my therapist, had been right all along. I wasn't a victim of life. I had the option of starting anything I wanted, Lord willing. "There's nothing I'd love more, Dad."

I had one more happy tear slip through my eyelashes. Looking at my watch, I still had two hours to get refreshed for my date, which I knew I would attend. I thanked my parents for their words and a few minutes later, we ended the call as I wished them well on their New Year's journey home from Alaska. My heart was full.

*****

An hour later, I was back at the boutique with Tamara.

"I wish I had something I could loan you, Claire. Nothing that fits me right now would work, obviously." She put a hand on her baby bump.

"Aww, you are so kind, Tamara. Don't worry, I have things that might work for you in my closet. I did go through the 'I've given up' phase many times in my life."

We both chuckled, only stopping when Tamara pulled out a silky, red dress. We gasped. "It's beautiful," I said, reaching for the price tag instinctively. Tamara swatted my hand away.

"Try it on first. Just for fun, if anything. You need to see how this makes you feel before you look at what it costs."

"Wise words, Tamara. Thank you."

The boutique manager led me to the small fitting area, unzipped the dress, and removed the safety pin that had the price tag on it. "Take your friend's advice," she said as she winked at me.

The dress had thick straps and came to right above my knee. The color was flawless; it made my skin glow and my hair look more strawberry than blonde. Between its sweetheart neckline and the gentle ruching down the sides, the dress was extremely flattering, creating a feminine hourglass shape. As I stood in the dress catching my reflection in the mirror, I knew it was special. I knew I wanted to wear it. Nothing else would hold a candle to it.

"Okay, okay. How much?" I whispered to Tamara as I tiptoed out of the dressing area, back in my clothes. The dress was still hanging inside. If I needed a second mortgage to get it, I didn't want to feel ashamed putting it back.

"It's not *that* bad. You'd spend more on a day skiing."

Had I expressed just how much I loved this woman? "With or without ski gear rentals?" I asked while she pondered.

"Like, if you had to buy the lift ticket, rent the gear, *and* buy some cute clothes to wear so you feel *good* about skiing, it would be under that price."

My ski pants were over a hundred dollars. How much were we talking? I held up my hand, holding out all five fingers in reference to the price.

"No, no. Not five hundred."

I held up three fingers.

She smiled sheepishly. "A teeny bit more. But the good news is, I brought high heels too. You know, in case while I was here at higher altitude, my feet would un-swell."

We laughed, and I hugged her, feeling better about things since looking at my job offer from Blake's father. I could swing the dress.

*****

When I turned the corner of the hallway and walked into the grand fireplace area, I saw Blake waiting there, hands in his pockets, looking out at the snow that had just begun gently falling. He hadn't seen me yet, so I took notice of the fondue pot sitting on the square table in the center of the couches with an assortment of fruits and cheesecake pieces. A single long-stemmed rose was lying beside it.

"Wowwww. Well, hello, gorgeous," Blake spoke, and I saw he could see my reflection in the glass as I entered the room. Spinning around, we walked towards each other, but I didn't know what to do when we got there. He took the lead and held my hands in his. "Happy New Year's," he spoke softly, appearing to be a little nervous. I felt his hands trembling in mine. "I'm so glad you made it."

"I almost didn't… But then, I did." I smiled ear to ear, knowing I made the right choice.

He looked me over respectfully. "That dress is everything. Have you ever been told that bright red is your color? It's also what you were wearing when we met."

"Oh yes, that's right. I was wearing my ski coat out since it hadn't gotten much wear before that." I smiled at him and noticed his impeccable outfit. He had changed since I saw him earlier in the day, putting on a collarless shirt with the top unbuttoned. He wore crisp, black slacks and a fitted blazer. I caught a glance of our reflection in the window. We looked like we went together, and I was happy to be there on that unexpected New Year's Eve date.

"Care for some fondue?" He motioned to the setup behind him, and when I agreed, he led me by my left hand to a seat. Two champagne flutes sat beside the plates. "Champagne?" He held up a beautiful festive bottle.

"I'd love to, but that stuff gives me a headache." I threw my hands up.

"Same here. I can't drink it at all. How about some cold press?" He pointed to another bottle on the table. "Just made. Fresh from 'The Squeezery' downtown, which I can't say with a straight face."

I laughed in agreement, and he poured the colorful turquoise juice drink. "Spirulina, to give it some festivity of its own." It was delicious and paired perfectly with the chocolate fondue I'd dipped a strawberry into.

"Thank you. This is really fun, Blake— the perfect end to my vacation."

"I'm so glad to hear that. I wanted you to have fun tonight."

And we did. After eating a copious amount of fruit and chocolate fondue, two glasses of cold-press, and a few bites of cheesecake, we had a few more minutes until ten.

Blake picked up the rose from the table. "Why do I feel like I'm on one of those reality dating shows?" He handed it to me. "Claire, will you take this beautiful, fragrant flower I received from the man passing them out in the lobby?"

I laughed and took it. "Of course, Blake. Thank you for the rose." I breathed in its delicate scent.

"Shall we go to the balcony? We want to get a good spot for the show."

I nodded in agreement. He picked up his coat, and it was then I realized I'd forgotten mine. But not a second passed before he put his coat around my shoulders.

"Won't you be cold?" He was still gently trembling, after all.

"No, your smile keeps me warm."

"In that case…" I grinned dramatically, showing all of my teeth like I was on an infomercial.

"Perfect. I feel warmer already." Blake opened the door to the balcony, leading us out. My high heels clicked loudly on the flagstone tile. To my surprise, only a few people had come for the fireworks. Blake must have noticed the same.

"There's a big party at that bar tonight— you know, where we met for the second time."

"I'm surprised you didn't want to go there, then? Maybe I could re-enact the fall in case there was anything you missed the first time." I crossed my arms and leaned on the wood railing, looking towards the mountains.

"Oh, I didn't miss a thing. But I knew it would be quieter here, and I was hoping to tell you one more thing that I didn't get to earlier."

"Okay, what is it, Blake?" I stood up from the railing and turned my body to face him.

"Remember how I told my parents that we weren't dating?" I nodded. "That was missing something. Well… I told them we weren't dating, yet."

My heart picked up the pace.

"You see, I've never met anyone like you. You make me feel like I'm alive for the first time, not running from my father's shadow. I may have kept away from relationships, but with you, that is impossible to do, Claire Riley. Truth is, ever since you slipped on the wet tile at Barn Door, I can't get you out of my mind."

My heart felt like it was going to beat out of my chest as he took a step toward me. "So, what part of the fall did it for you? Was it my legs flying up in front of me, or… something else?"

He smiled and shook his head, taking my face in his hands. "It was your smile, Claire. How you held it— you didn't miss a beat; you didn't let it faze you. We all fall in life; I slipped just a few hours ago, in fact. Kind of did something to my knee. But you, Claire, did it with grace."

I was relishing in the fact that someone considered anything about me graceful, when he suddenly leaned in, still holding my face. "Truth is, I knew right at that moment who I was made for. My soul recognized yours."

As soon as his plush lips touched mine, the fireworks went off in my heart and in the sky.

Epilogue

"How about this?" My assistant, Lacey, came waddling by with a faux plant that was larger than she was. "I was thinking right here, in the corner." As she set the large pot down, she returned to her normal walk. "It creates a little height to the room, and that added texture is so lovely."

"It's perfect. Can we get a few more of these– for the private lounges? I really like your eye for detail." I high-fived Lacey, and she picked up her phone and made a call to secure more of the plants.

"They will have them here in one hour since they have them in their warehouse already, so everything will be set for tomorrow."

The final walk-through was that night, so that worked great for both our timeline and the grand opening of

Sage Mountain's new luxury airport. The ribbon cutting would be at 10 a.m. with our first flight arriving at noon. I could barely contain my excitement.

The plants arrived just as she said they would, and once they were in, we knew our work there was done. "I couldn't have done it without you all," I spoke to my team, as I had become the manager of five designers. They were all extraordinary in different ways.

Angelo was the guru of paint colors, trims, and wallpaper. Though I'd always been indifferent to the latter because of my preference for bold artwork instead of busy walls, he'd opened my eyes to a different kind of style.

Paulette was the Jill of all trades. A furniture restorer in her time off, she often sold me custom pieces from her own shop. For that project, we had many of her end tables in our lounges that were made from old whiskey barrels.

Trevor was my contractor. He worked with every person there to execute the collective vision, but often he had the best eye out of the group. His knowledge of materials had been immensely helpful as we created a space that would last for decades.

Sybil was our art curator. My favorite thing to do was give her a one-word description of a space, and then she would somehow find the biggest and most beautiful art for it. Even when I'd been nervous about a piece– for instance, the larger-than-life surrealist Elk watercolor she brought in for a private lounge– once it went on the wall, it was clear nothing else could ever compare. Sybil was a master at what she did, and I reminded her of that every day.

Last but not least, my personal favorite was Lacey. She and I got to work side-by-side making spaces magical. She was quick to become my best friend as well, and we were each other's personal cheerleaders for everything.

The group gathered up before I sent everyone home for the evening, as I had an announcement to make. "I've just heard back from the board of directors that our bonuses have been approved. You'll see those in your next paychecks."

To survive in a town like this, we all relied on having a steady income, and I promised my team I would go to bat for them every time, a promise I had followed through on. As they cheered and hugged one another, I told them to all go home and enjoy time with their loved ones. "I'll see you tomorrow at the ribbon cutting ceremony."

As they all turned to leave, I called out, "Lacey, wait up! We have just enough time to grab some dinner before things get crazy. Shall I take us to get some sushi?"

Lacey ecstatically obliged, and we left together.

Over sashimi and miso soup, Lacey and I got down to business, but not the kind that involved wallpaper or throw pillow textures. I began, "So… you sent me that cryptic text last night that you think you are falling in love with someone, but you haven't told me who he is. Are you planning on elaborating on that anytime soon?" I put my fist under my chin while I waited for her to answer. Under the dim lights, it appeared she was blushing as she floundered her answer.

"Not just yet. I want to be sure that it's mutual. It would be so embarrassing if I was totally wrong about this, and he's just wanting to be my platonic friend. Or worse, he sees me as a sister, like the last one *whose name shall not be spoken.*"

I nodded, understanding her hesitancy, considering how things had gone south with her last crush, Jack, but I wasn't satisfied with that answer. I was still needing more information. "Okay," taking a sip of my miso soup out of its square ladle, "It has to be someone I know… But I'm thinking there's more to it than that. Is it... someone we work with?" I gave her a coy smirk, and she gave in, instantly blurting it out.

"It's Trevor! I feel like I've gone mad. If this were the nineteenth century, I'd be committed. I am head-over-heels in love with a man I've barely had the strength to speak to, let alone make direct eye contact with. I've made it known in every way I can in my mind without speaking it aloud. If he doesn't ask me out soon, I may just die from the agony."

I didn't have the heart to tell her that Trevor had walked in five minutes before while she was in the back washing her hands. It hadn't crossed my mind to tell her that beforehand because the interaction was so brief, and after all, it was a place we all frequented multiple times a week. Thankfully, I didn't have to tell her anything, as Trevor stood up from a table out of eyesight, but not earshot.

"Lacey…" Trevor was smiling, but the nerves in his face made me feel like I was watching someone cross a tightrope with no safety precautions.

"Trevor, I– you, me– " Lacey was fumbling her words like a bouncy ball. I had never seen her so nervous about something in her life, but I was proud that she wasn't running away from this scenario either. She was taking it head on.

"Can I take you to dinner, Lacey?" Trevor reached for her hand, and I realized my cue to leave had arrived.

"Darn it!" I hollered. "If I don't leave right now, I won't have enough time to stop by my condo and change before I meet with the board. Lacey, is it okay if I go?"

She looked at me with wide eyes and smiled as I slid out of the booth, and Trevor swiftly took my place. As I went to the front counter to pay for what we had ordered, I saw the waitress deliver Trevor's tray of food to where he was sitting with Lacey, and it seemed that they were in an easy conversation. What an unexpected coupling, but it made sense to me. Trevor was thoughtful and kind. Lacey was sweet and endearing and both of them were bookish, quiet types. I could hear her laughter bellowing, and I loved this for her.

*****

That evening, at 6 p.m. prompt, I met the board of directors and James Walker at the front door of the airport for our final walkthrough. "Good evening, James." I greeted him first with a firm handshake. He gave me a warm smile and thanked me for all the work I'd done on the design.

"It was a major collaborative effort. The team you've given me is incredible. We all work together for one vision, and I've never experienced anything quite so unified before. I don't know where you find all of these people."

As I beamed about my amazing co-workers, I held the door open and everyone else walked inside with James and me the last to enter. "Good evening, everyone. I see a few new faces here. I am Claire Riley, the senior design consultant. I am so blessed to be standing here in our beautiful new airport! We have some drinks and hors d'oeuvre over in our reception area afterwards. Follow me and let me show you what we've accomplished."

The walkthrough took an hour, and we had a wonderful reception afterwards. Everyone was pleased with the final look of the new airport. After another hour of mingling with the board, I excused myself and went home, falling asleep the moment my head hit the pillow.

The next morning, I was up at dawn drinking coffee and reading my devotional. Jesus had freed me from the insecurities of my mind that led me to idolizing the people I admired. Ever since I realized what a dangerous path I'd been on, I actively made sure that only God was my front and center. He was the only one I'd aim to please while loving those around me at a healthy level.

When I was finished, I went to my window and prayed over the day. Since I could see the airport from my second story condo along with the beautiful gondolas riding up to their peaks and valleys, I thanked the Lord for giving me such blessings that I could stay in the only home I'd ever known: Sage Mountain, Wyoming.

I had planned to wear a sharp pantsuit to the ribbon cutting ceremony, but the morning of, I pulled out a light blue dress that I'd been wanting to wear at some point along with its matching blue heels. The woman at the boutique had raved about the color complimenting my eyes, and I agreed with her. It made me feel beautiful and feminine. I wore a modest set of rose gold jewelry and just enough makeup to make my eyelashes and lips show up, as they felt otherwise invisible in my features.

Theo was seldom thought of those days, but I did see his updates online from time to time. He had gone on his Canadian adventure with SkySki and placed first in the overall ski jump for his category, which happened to be the qualifier for something else. Yep, Theo was going to the Olympics the next year in Argentina.

I couldn't be any happier for him but for reasons that did not relate to skiing. Before he went to Canada, he announced on his socials that he'd given his life to Christ. Then, a month later, he posted an invitation to a ski-jumping introduction that doubled as a men's fellowship. He had begun using his gift of sport and his social platforms to reach others and bring them to Jesus. It was beautiful.

Aside from that, his love life was also on the up. He met a Canadian woman, Fern, at one of his competitions, and they were engaged. It happened fast, but it was clear that they were meant to be together. She was a tall brunette with honey eyes and quite lovely from what online persona I'd seen. The funny thing was… She didn't ski. I guessed Theo finally found what he was looking for that had nothing to do with snow and everything to do with love.

As for Tara, she had become one of my closest (and most unexpected) friends. She had reached out to me after New Year's about a program on Friday afternoons called *"Ski Sisters Club,"* that was a women's group focused on bettering our skills on skis. I jumped at the chance and with Tara's assistance and God's provisions, I had nothing but enjoyable experiences. She did end up with her cute co-worker, the fellow instructor, to no one's surprise. Their chemistry was off the charts, and she hilariously interviewed his friends after they started dating to make sure he wasn't already in a relationship.

Clicking my heels through my condo, I grabbed a light jacket on my way out. My father had made good on his suggestion and had personally replaced his Wheaties poster with a belated Christmas gift: a large gold mirror that made my space feel bigger and gave an incredible amount of light into the room. It became my favorite part of my living room. The shelf by my window newly held a dozen photos of my day-to-day life, including one from the wonderful getaway weekend that I spent with my parents in Cork's Canyon after New Year's. The best part about it? Blake came with us, too. And they absolutely loved him… just like I did.

While Blake lived in Denver full-time, he had been commuting every other week to see me for over three months until he bought a beautiful little bungalow in downtown Sage Mountain. It was just mere steps from the Pine Needle gondola, which happened to be his favorite lift. When we went to tour the home, he asked me if I could see myself living there. I looked around the place with a critical eye, pointing out the discolored walls, small entryways, and dated tile. Of course, I was totally just playing the game, which he knew. I loved the house, and it had amazing potential. It was modest but centrally located to everything in town. He put in an offer right away as the market there had been booming. His offer was accepted the same day instead of starting a bidding war with no end in sight. He couldn't wait to tell me the news. "It's meant to be, Claire."

Blake's plan was to continue to work remotely as the financial advisor for the company until he finished the offices for those who wished to relocate. They were being built on a parcel adjacent to the airport. With Blake's real passion being in real estate, it was a perfect fit and great for my team as well since we were designing them. His father approved the opening of the new Wyoming branch for the company, which created many jobs for those who still remained in Sage Mountain. To them, James became a household name under much better pretenses.

With Blake's future plans involving his move to Wyoming and his father's plans to pass the company down to him, Blake had taken time to think about what he wanted to do in his life and what it meant for his father. Ultimately, when his father retired the next year, he would be handing the company to Blake, but it would be run by a new CEO of Blake's choosing. Blake had told me that it was because of me that he had decided he would take the reins. When we met, he realized he had been running from something because of the implications of his needing to be married and having yet to meet the right partner. That frightened him. But in the end, his father saw what an independent man Blake was with or without a family. Plus, he had the desire for a family but was wise enough not to jump into the wrong relationship. After they had a heart-to-heart on the matter, James' previous reasoning no longer held any weight.

As I arrived at the ribbon cutting, I was pleased the wind had died down, and the sun provided us some warmth. It was a beautiful late spring day for new beginnings. The first people I recognized were Mickey, Tamara, and their new beautiful baby, Elsie Eileen.

"Well, hello, baby! How are you? Are you loving every outfit I've gotten you? Maybe not yet, but you will, I promise. And I'll tell you a secret: Your dad might think he's the man of the house, but you are the one who rules the roost, little lady. Anything you ask for, he's going to get for you."

"Gee, thanks, Claire. She already has my heart, every inch of our home is dedicated to her life, and now she knows my bank account is at her fancy, too?"

I hugged Tamara and Mickey while we playfully bantered. "I'm telling you, she's the prettiest baby I've ever seen. She's going to figure all this out eventually– might as well save her the trouble, Mick."

At just a week old, she was wearing a bright yellow coat and generously swaddled in luxurious blankets while lying in a stroller that looked more like a bassinet on wheels.

"You didn't have to come today, but I'm so glad you did."

Tamara flashed her bright smile but yawned shortly after. "I needed the fresh air. It's just such a gorgeous day. Besides, Mickey wanted to show off his new baby."

"And, and, and— don't forget, my baby momma." Mickey wrapped his arm around Tamara and kissed her forehead.

"Thank you, all three of you, for being here for me today! I can't wait for you to see the design. In fact, I think you'll especially like the throw pillows in the lounges because they remind me of the ones in your house."

Tamara was nodding along, but clearly, exhaustion was catching up. Just then, another car came up, and I recognized the style of driving. The only person who circled the parking lot three times before parking was my mother.

"I better go greet my parents."

My parents finally parked after I walked away from Mickey and Tamara, and I went to them so I could give them a hug. To my surprise, Blake was getting out of their back seat.

"Guess who took us out for breakfast today?" my mother beamed. I looked at Blake with wonderment. He didn't let me think too long, as he leaned in for a kiss, telling me how much he loved my dress.

"Good morning, blue eyes. Look how great this color is on you." He held my hands out from a distance, so he could get a good look. Both of my parents agreed.

"Well thanks, guys. Aren't you too sweet?" We walked back to the entrance as I remembered I needed to grab the ribbon inside. James, Blake's dad, would hold one end, and the president of the board, John, would hold the other end, while my father would cut the ribbon with a large pair of shiny, silver scissors. Being Sage Mountain's own Olympian came with some real perks. "I better go fetch the ribbon. I'll be right back."

My mother chirped up, "I'll go with you, Claire." She walked with me inside, and the moment we were out of eyesight, she took my arm. "Claire." Her smile went from ear to ear, and I held my breath waiting for the words. "Blake wanted to take us to breakfast this morning."

"Yeah? That's what you said. How sweet of him. I really do love that man." I opened the supplies closet door that was a catch all for everything we needed out of the way and looked through the bins for the ribbon that Lacey had put in there last week.

"Because he wanted to speak to us."

I froze in my tracks. "And?" She had my full attention now.

"And… I'm not telling. But I just wanted you to know that we approve."

I shrugged so hard in confusion that my chin disappeared into my neck. Then it dawned on me. Did he ask for their blessing? We clicked in a way I didn't know was possible, pretty much from the moment we met. But once we started dating, for real that is, it felt like a fairytale.

"Here it is, sweetie."

My mother pulled out a giant roll of red ribbon and the shiny silver pair of scissors. I robotically walked back to the front of the airport as the excitement seeped through my body. Looking at Blake, I thanked God for sending me such a kind, loving man into my life. He exuded patience and understanding, which had taught me so much. Blake inspired me to live to the fullest and encouraged me to do anything that I wanted to do, which turned out, was to ski.

Dating the future CEO of snow had some perks, such as the free ski passes to any resort we wanted. While Blake had certainly traveled on his own dime, the skiing was almost always included, and he had been already eagerly planning our trips for next season. Just the week before, he excitedly called to ask me my thoughts on a cross-country trip to spend one day at each resort. "We could get a souvenir from each place. You know, like a snow globe or something. Then one day, we could get a curio cabinet to display them all. What do you think?"

I laughed. "Or, what about a sticker at each place? We could create some kind of motif of them on canvas– a little easier to display."

"That's why you are the brains of this operation, Claire."

He was always coming up with fun ideas for us and was just a joy to be around. With Blake, everything was easy, lighthearted. Our love didn't feel superficial or based on any pretenses. We knew exactly who the other was and wholly accepted each other.

Only through my trials was I able to give up the parts of myself that kept me from fully knowing Jesus, and through them, I found the love He intended for me to have.

My mind returned to the task at hand as I held the large roll of red, silky ribbon. A group had formed on the flagstone entrance in my absence. It looked like everyone in Sage Mountain was in attendance. I saw my team, scanning them for Lacey and Trevor who, to the joy of my heart, were holding hands. Blake and I personally looked into any rules about dating while working at the same company and were proud to report there was nothing in the book saying we couldn't, while Blake had assured me if there was, he would use his powers to change that.

Everyone gathered for the ribbon cutting photo op. On that unusually warm April day as I looked out at the beautiful mountain scape that would soon be filled with summer wildflowers in every color of the rainbow, I was at peace. The sun was sparkling in the bright blue sky, and I closed my eyes as I felt the warmth kiss my face. God was so good all the time. As Blake took my hand while my father cut the ribbon, I felt myself longing for winter to return.

Acknowledgments

Thank you, God, for instilling a passion for writing within my soul. Though I spent much of my life running in the wrong direction, from the moment I was saved, I have been writing for You.

Many friends have made this book possible, especially two brilliant authors whom I admire. Jessica— thank you for letting me bounce countless ideas off you and for analyzing so many of my drafts, cover ideas, and the endless slew of titles. Cali— thank you for meeting me where I am and for your constant encouragement to keep going. Writing is not for the faint-hearted, and you both have been authoring fantastic books of your own while cheering me on.

Thank you to my editor, Ronda, for her incredible work in navigating my many, many errors. Your polish is exactly what this manuscript needed.

To my readers- thank you for embracing these stories and the characters within them. I am grateful for every moment you spend within these pages.

And finally, to my husband, Chad— thank you for your unwavering support as I pursue my dreams of becoming a novelist.

About the Author

Cassandra discovered her passion for writing at the age of seven when she purchased a diary at the Scholastic Book Fair. What began with journal entries about her school and home life later evolved into a collection of poems, short stories, and novels.

Her hobbies include skiing, traveling around the Rocky Mountains, and reading. Much of her writing inspiration stems from her love of dogs, her Onondaga heritage, and her Christian faith.

Cassandra's favorite genres of books are Christian fiction novels, Thrillers, and anything British.

She is a full-time writer and resides in the mountains of Wyoming with her husband, Chad.

Other Books

Also by Cassandra Joelle-

Book 1 in the 'Dog-Mom Rom-Com' Series:

A New Leash on Life

Get ready for a hilarious Christian romantic comedy as we follow the journey of a thirty-something introverted woman, Katie Fitzgerald, who's longing for a husband. But when she accidentally adopts a dog, she discovers that love comes in unexpected ways, and that God's timing is always perfect.

Genre: Christian Romantic Comedy/Women's Fiction.

Stay tuned for the anticipated sequel as the second installment of the 'Dog-Mom Rom-Com' series, *Fetching Love,* is releasing in early 2025!

The Curse of Josephine Bagley-
Over the course of a century, three individuals are woven together by a decades-old curse:

William, after surviving an Indian raid on his orphanage due to his facial disfigurement, goes on to live among the tribe. But when misfortune befalls them, he is quickly traded away and faced with a pivotal choice that changes his life forever.

Josephine has faced immense loss. Despite her granddaughter's efforts to help her find solace in faith, she finds she can't let go of the past and falls further into her belief that she's eternally bound to darkness.

Saraphina, a fledgling antiques dealer, gets the surprise of her life when a courier delivers notice that she's the last surviving relative of the Bagley Estate. What seemed like a windfall that could help her career now causes her to question her own reality.

In this tale of intertwining mystery, loss, and faith, these souls navigate through nefarious trials to find the gift of grace and forgiveness that extends to us all.

Genre: Christian Gothic